flowers *on the* milkstool

THE DIARY OF MARY LAWSON
BY TABI RAE

TATE PUBLISHING, LLC

ↆ.

Published in the United States of America
by Tate Publishing, LLC
127 East Trade Center Terrace
Mustang, OK 73064
(888) 361-9473

ISBN: 1-5988655-2-8

060606

Dedication

For Mama, the woman who inspires me to greatness just by the way she lives her life. You've been by my side every step of the way, and I could never thank you enough. With all of my love, I dedicate this book to you.

Wednesday, April 5, 1871

Today is my fourteenth birthday. Mama and Papa gave me this diary as my gift. It was Papa's idea. You see, I have seven brothers and no sisters. Now, I will have a place to tell about my life. First, I will tell of my brothers.

Three of my brothers are older than I am. Ben is the eldest at nineteen. He is very protective over me, and I love him very much. He is courting Penny Walker, and I have no doubt they will be married soon. Samuel is eighteen. He's quiet and thoughtful, and always seems to be looking off into the distance. He doesn't like to work, and I think he regrets being born on a farm. Luke is fifteen and unruly, always being brought home hurt or half-dead, but he's always fine. He teases me often, but never really hurts me.

After three sons, I was born, the only daughter. One year after me, Jonah came along; the first of four more sons (much to Mama's delight). Jonah is much like Luke, though not as mature. Jonah was followed by Micah, who is eleven. He tries to do what the other boys do, but sometimes he isn't bold or strong enough. Danny is eight, and the sweetest boy I've ever known. I love him dearly. Levi is the youngest at three, and I think he will be like Luke and Jonah.

That leaves me. I'm Mary, the lone daughter of David and Jane Lawson. Mama told me once that Mary means bitterness, and I think that's what she felt when I was born. Mama only wanted sons.

People usually think I am rough and tumble, like boys, but I'm not. I am meek, shy, and quiet. However, I am very strong. Farm work can make anyone strong. Work leaves little time for anything else, but I will make time to record things in my diary every day.

Thursday, April 6, 1871

Since nothing worth writing about happened today, I will tell what I look like. My hair is dark and curly, and reaches only to my shoulders. It's very unmanageable, and I keep it braided all the time. My eyes are brown. I'm very plain, of average height, and I'm lean and slender. I have freckles on my face from working in the sun my entire life. I fear that, looking the way I do, I will never be very attractive. I'm only a farm girl.

Friday, April 7, 1871

We awoke to a frost this morning. Papa roused everyone out of bed in order to save the corn, the only crop that has been planted yet. We had to pour water over fields and fields of tiny sprouts before the sun came up and killed them. Since there were nine people working, excluding Levi, we saved all of the corn. In addition to the corn, we will also plant wheat and many vegetables in Mama's garden. We also have livestock to care for. All of these things make up our livelihood. That's why we live in Kansas.

Later—

It is very late, and everyone is asleep, except for me. I am in my small room, lit only by a single candle. Because I am the only daughter in the family, I have my own room. All of the boys sleep in the spacious attic. Mama and Papa have a regular bedroom. Levi used to sleep on the trundle bed in their room, just like all of the babies did, but he moved up to the attic a few weeks ago.

My room was added to the side of the house, much like a lean-to. It has a small door and only enough room for my bed, a tiny table, and hooks for my dresses to hang on. It's a wonderful place for me to be alone when I want to be. Sometimes, it's a place to escape from my brothers. Though I would like to write all night, I must get some sleep.

Saturday, April 8, 1871

I awoke early this morning to milk the cows. Ben calls me Mary the milk maid. Since it's my job to milk the cows, I suppose that is exactly what I am. We have ten cows, and much more milk than our family needs, so we sell what we don't need. The cows behave well with me, and I do a very good job of milking them. Danny comes with me sometimes, watching as the milk fills the pail. He and I both like feeling the warmth of the cows breaking through the coolness of the morning. Danny never says a word, and never has. His smile warms my heart, and his eyes speak a thousand words. In these mornings, I talk to Danny, trying to coax a word from him, but I never do. Every day, I pray he will gain his speech. He has a very sharp mind, and learns quickly. He spends much of his time with me, and I watch over him diligently. Papa talks to Danny often, taking him into town and on errands. Mama talks to him sometimes, but doesn't seem to know what to say. I feel bad for Mama sometimes.

Sunday, April 9, 1871

Church today. After cleaning up and scrubbing my little brothers' faces, we all piled into the wagon for the ride into town for church services. Though I love God

very much, church and Sundays bore me. I'm glad today is over.

Monday, April 10, 1871

Mama added tomatoes to her garden today. She tends to it faithfully, and tries to keep Levi out of the plants. Papa works the fields; all of the boys help him, and sometimes I do too. Luke gets lazy sometimes, and this makes Papa angry. Papa is a hardworking man, with broad shoulders, a strong back, and a big heart. He won't tolerate laziness from anyone, especially his own children.

Tuesday, April 11, 1871

Mr. Walker came to see Papa today. Mr. Walker's farm is several miles from ours. He brought along his daughter, Penny, who Ben is courting. Penny is a pretty girl, blonde and blue-eyed. Papa and Mr. Walker talked for some time, mostly about farming, but their conversation always turns to the war. Both fought together in the Confederate Army. Papa never talks about it with us. I only remember that he was gone for a long time, but returned the same as when he left. Mr. Walker returned with a limp.

Wednesday, April 12, 1871

Micah came home from the fields today with a tear in his pant's leg and an enormous scrape on his shin. I led him into the house, watching as he held back his tears. He had been standing too close when Jonah swung the hoe. Mama bandaged his leg, fussing at him for not being careful.

"You're old enough to be careful, but too childish and not strong enough to practice your good sense!" Mama told him, sending him outside.

I felt bad for Micah. He is strong, and it's easy to get hurt in the fields. Frontier life isn't easy. Mama thinks everyone is as strong as she thinks she is, though Mama was raised as a southern belle. She married Papa, a frontiersman, because she loved him and because she wanted adventure. I think she found it. Eight children is an adventure. I know Mama is very strong, but at times she isn't very understanding.

Thursday, April 13, 1871

Micah's leg is a little better, but it will take a while for it to heal.

Friday, April 14, 1871

Worked in the fields today. We have a large amount of property. Right now, it must be plowed and planted. Papa drives the horses to plow the fields, and we follow behind him, planting seeds and throwing out rocks. The work is hard, but I enjoy being with my brothers. Ben is a joker and keeps us laughing. Danny brings us water when the sun gets hot. Mama made a wonderful lunch at noon, then we head back into the fields. Sometimes, Mama makes a fuss because we are doing the job of slaves. Mama is a firm believer in slavery since that is what she was raised to believe. Papa, however, doesn't believe in

slavery. I don't believe in it either. Why should we force someone to do work that we can do on our own? I'm glad that I have Papa's beliefs (as well as his accent).

Saturday, April 15, 1871

Mama and I were cleaning after breakfast this morning when Mama's face grew very pale. Suddenly, she dashed out the door, getting sick. I brought her back into the house and helped her to her rocking chair. I asked if she was all right, and she smiled.

"I'm expecting another baby," she said, and I suddenly focused on the small roundness of her belly. I hadn't noticed. She should deliver around October. I pray for a sister.

Sunday, April 16, 1871

Mama was feeling very sick this morning, so Papa and the boys went to church alone. Mama allowed me to stay with her. We talked more today than I believe we ever have. Mama confided in me that she has a bad feeling about the baby. She feels fearful, a sense of foreboding. I have learned one thing: Mama's feelings are rarely wrong. We prayed for Mama and the baby. For the first time, I saw something in Mama's eyes that I've never seen before. She looked afraid, like the fire in her eyes had been snuffed out. It scared me.

Monday, April 17, 1871

I was nearly finished milking our ten cows this morning when Ben ran into the barn excitedly. He wanted

me to come with him; he had something to show me. First, I finished the milking, putting the milk away and cleaning the pails. Then Ben led me out to our pasture. My favorite mare had just given birth to a beautiful foal. My brothers were already gathered around. We stood in the morning dew, in awe of the new life before us. I thought again about Mama's baby, and said another prayer. The work of the day began, but I went to see the foal as often as I could. He's very beautiful, and I love horses anyway. I can ride just as well as any of the boys, but I don't ride like a lady would. I'm a farm girl; I'm allowed to ride with one leg on each side of the horse. Papa allows me to, as long as Mama doesn't know about it.

Tuesday, April 18, 1871

Mama sent Danny and me into town to get eggs. We have no chickens of our own. Danny and I walked the three miles to town. When we arrived, we went to the general store. Mr. Bailey owns it; he's a very nice man. He greeted us, and gave Danny a piece of candy. He put a dozen eggs in the basket I had, talking all the while. I answered his questions about Papa, Mama, the boys, and the farm, while Danny stood and smiled. I enjoy going to town, though I'm unsure of people I don't know. Familiar people make me very comfortable, but I'm too shy around strangers. I'm just not as brave as I should be.

Wednesday, April 19, 1871

Mama can hardly eat. She is sick every day, and very weak. I told her she should see the doctor, but she refuses. She feels it will pass soon. I've been caring for

things more often so Mama can rest. Danny and Micah help in the house, and Jonah would too if he didn't break things so easily.

Thursday, April 20, 1871

This morning, Mama became very ill and went straight to bed. Papa was already in the fields with the boys. I sent Danny to get him, telling him to run. I stayed with Mama, trying to help her feel better, but she looked so sick. It seemed to take Papa forever to arrive. When he did, I begged him to make Mama go see the doctor. Papa disagreed, saying that the doctor should come here. I volunteered to get one of the boys to ride for the doctor, but Papa had another plan.

"It will take too long to get one of the boys," he said, for they were all in the field. "You get a horse and ride for the doctor, and hurry! Your mother is very ill!"

Papa's tone frightened me. I ran to the barn, placed a bridle over one of the horses and rode off without a saddle. I pushed the horse to gallop as fast as he could, and I arrived in town quickly. People stared at me as I galloped to the doctor's office. I prayed he was there as I pounded on the door. When he answered, I explained about Mama, and he hurried off on my horse to save time. I was already breathless, but I ran all the way home. I arrived to find Papa anxiously waiting while the doctor looked after Mama. Papa held Levi in his lap, and was obviously praying for Mama. The doctor reported that Mama is simply overworked and is to stay in bed for a few days. I am relieved that all she needs is rest in order to get well. The baby will be fine as well. I am still praying for a sister.

Friday, April 21, 1871

I cooked every meal today. Mama seems to like the idea of being able to stay in bed for a few days. Mama was raised as a lady and was waited on by servants. I'm not sure if her idea of adventure when she married Papa included having to work. That may have come as a surprise. I'm used to it.

Saturday, April 22, 1871

As we ate breakfast this morning, Ben asked to call on Penny Walker. Papa agreed, for he approves of the match. Mama isn't as happy. She's reluctant to give up one of her sons, even in marriage.

Monday, April 24, 1871

The boys went swimming today. I couldn't go with them because I am a girl. Therefore, I went for a walk on the prairie. As I walked, I saw a covered wagon pulling across the prairie. The driver saw me and waved, so I waited for them to approach. As they did, I looked them over. A young man and woman (with a very round belly) rode on the wagon seat, and a younger man on a horse. They all looked tired and dusty. However, they were pleasant when they reached where I was standing. They said their last name is Hamilton, and they were looking for the old Williams farm. I told them it was nearly two miles past our farm. I invited them to come and have dinner with us, and they happily agreed. The young woman told me to climb into the back of the wagon. When I did, I found another young girl with red hair, blue eyes, and a pleasant smile. Her name is Sarah, and she is fourteen like me. She is traveling with her two older brothers. The other woman is her sister-in-law, her oldest brother's wife. Papa and Mama welcomed them, as did my brothers.

Sarah and I immediately became friends. Her oldest brother, Lyle, and his wife Nora are settling onto the old Williams farm (the Williams family moved away years ago). I like them very much. Sarah will live with them, for her parents died years ago. Her other brother, Rob, is sixteen and handsome. He and Luke already dislike one another. The Hamilton's left for their farm after dinner, but Sarah promised to visit soon. I can't express how wonderful it is to have a girl my age living close to me!

Tuesday, April 25, 1871

Sarah came to visit today. We didn't talk very much yesterday, but I don't talk very much anyway. She is much bolder than I am, and I like her very much. Since Papa doesn't have much work to do in the fields right now, we are allowed to do other things. I went with Sarah to her new house and saw how it had fallen into disrepair. Lyle and Rob were working on the roof while Nora was sweeping the floor. I volunteered to help, and found myself working until sundown. I found it pleasant to be in a different place for the day. Sarah has a very nice family. I told her to visit me any time she wants to. She told me that she and I are going to be best friends. I believe it as well!

Wednesday, April 26, 1871

The doctor returned today. He told Mama she could go back to working, but not do anything too difficult. It's good news; I can't do all of the things Mama can.

Thursday, April 27, 1871

Papa brought news today that outlaws have been roaming the area. This struck fear in my heart. What might outlaws do to people? We certainly have no money to give them (or for them to steal). I pray God protects us.

Saturday, April 29, 1871

I spent the day out in the sun. Sarah and I don't play like we would if we were younger; we are young ladies. However, we do have a good time. We sit in the prairie grass, watching the boys and talking. Danny brings us flowers and tiny animals he finds in the grass. Danny can coax any animal to trust him. Ben went to see Penny, so I didn't see him very much today. Samuel sits in the shade of a nearby cluster of trees, drawing what he sees. Levi usually plays in the grass, making up his own games. Micah and Jonah spend much of the day together. Jonah always has to be better than Micah at everything. Today, Luke and Rob went hunting, and it appears they may become friends after all. I love summer so. It's a time when work seems fun and the sun shines longer during the day.

Monday, May 1, 1871

I went to town with Papa today. He treated me like a grown woman, and I walked with my hand on his arm. I even pinned my hair atop my head, with Mama's help. Of course, my bonnet was covering my hair. Papa was only going to the general store to get parts for his other wagon, but it was a wonderful trip for me. I felt very special. Papa can make anyone feel special.

As we were leaving town, I saw a group of rough-looking men ride into town. They stopped at the saloon, and I wondered if they were the outlaws. I'm thankful we don't live in town where such people gather.

Tuesday, May 2, 1871

Mama is feeling much better. The fire has returned to her eyes, and cheer to her voice. I have missed having her well. And everyone missed her cooking, a skill which I do not possess. I still have much to learn.

Wednesday, May 3, 1871

Luke came home with a black eye and a bloody nose. He had been in a fight with Rob. He wouldn't say why they were fighting, but Mama and Papa were very upset. Luke was forbidden to leave the farm alone for a week. He has gotten into a lot of trouble this time.

Thursday, May 4, 1871

Mr. Walker came to visit today. He told Papa that he and his family are moving to California. Ben was listening, and he knew as well as I did that Penny is leaving, too. I'm in my room now, listening. Ben is talking to Mama and Papa, trying to convince them to allow him to marry Penny and go with them. Mama can't bear the idea of parting with her eldest son. Papa thinks it's a fine idea, but wants to know that Ben is sure, and if Penny will agree. They are beginning to speak a little softer, but Ben is still making his point. I'm sure they'll have reached a decision by morning.

Friday, May 5, 1871

At breakfast, Ben announced he intends to marry Penny Walker. He went to ask her, and returned to say that she agreed. They plan to be married tomorrow, and Mama is planning a small celebration and farewell after the wedding. I don't want Ben to leave, but I know that he loves Penny. Mr. Walker refused to approve of the marriage unless Ben goes to California with them, and Ben agreed. I will miss him. We'll all miss him. Hopefully, he will write letters telling of California. I would never be brave enough to leave home, but I would love to see other places.

Saturday, May 6, 1871

Ben and Penny were married today. Only Mama, Papa, and Mr. and Mrs. Walker went to the church with them. Afterward, a celebration was held at our house. Neighbors came from all around, and so many women came to cook that Sarah and I were able to spend the day in leisure. The food was plentiful, and everyone ate their fill. As dusk fell, the music began. I love dancing to the music of fiddles. Papa danced with me because Mama wasn't feeling well enough to dance. I also danced with Ben, and Luke even danced with me once. Samuel never dances, and the younger boys don't know how to dance yet. They spend their time playing. Jonah picks on the little neighbor girls, but stops if he's caught. Sarah danced with Luke once, having the ability to match his spirited movements. Rob asked me to dance, but I refused. I don't like him very much. He is arrogant and assuming. He wants everyone to think he is brave, but I think he is just stupid. Sarah is annoyed by him at times, too. She knows the difficulty of having brothers.

Sarah and I watched everyone dance after we became too tired. Ben and Penny left before everyone else, but not before Ben said goodbye to his family. I almost cried. I don't know when we'll ever see him again. I will pray for him every day.

Sunday, May 7, 1871

We went to church. Mama allowed me to sit with Sarah. Sarah was nearly making me laugh, imitating the preacher during his sermon. It was all I could do to keep from laughing out loud. If Mama had been nearby, I probably would have gotten into trouble. Never in my life would I have dared to act that way in church! Sarah is much bolder than I'll ever be.

Wednesday, May 10, 1871

The past three days have been terrible. Monday evening, Levi was missing. We couldn't find him any-where. A little boy can easily become lost on the wide prairie. Everyone began to look for him, calling his name. I searched everywhere I could think to look. Mama was in a panic. Papa and the boys were out searching. I took Danny and ran all the way to Sarah's house. I asked if anyone had seen Levi, and received a negative answer. Lyle and Rob immediately set out to help search, and Nora promised to watch for him as she went to comfort Mama. Sarah, Danny, and I searched until nightfall, then went home. Danny went straight to sleep, and Sarah and I slept in the barn, so as to hear if he had been found. I imagined many things that could have happened to Levi. I even considered the outlaws may have taken him, but I didn't

know why they would have. Tuesday brought no success. An entire day of searching and praying brought no news. Everyone we know was helping in the search. Still, the day went by and poor little Levi spent another day and night outside and alone. This morning, our fear grew deeper when we found that Danny was missing as well. Mama fainted and was carried to bed, attended to by Nora. I was at my wit's end, and Sarah was trying to comfort me.

Around noon, Danny returned, running as fast as he could through the prairie grass. Papa saw him coming and ran to meet him. It was strange the way Danny acted; he tugged at Papa's hand, pulling him in the direction he had come from. Papa followed, and I waited, somehow knowing that Danny knew where Levi was. It was true. A few hours later, Papa returned with Levi in his arms. Mama was awake by now and overjoyed, holding Levi close. Levi had spent the past days in a deep, dry creek bed, unable to climb back out. Papa spread the word that Levi had been found, and the tired searchers went home. Sarah went home too, but will come tomorrow. I held Danny close in my lap. I don't know how Danny knew, but I believe he knows things that others will never know. Though he can't speak, I believe God has given him a greater gift.

Thursday, May 11, 1871

The joy at our farm was very great this morning. Everyone was so pleased to see Levi rested and eating well, just like his usual self. As the day progressed, Levi didn't seem to be any different than he was before. Mama is as pleased as she can be. The loss of a child would be too much for her to bear. Sarah came today, and she and I walked across the prairie. We picked a few wildflowers,

enjoying their fragrance. I can't tell how wonderful it is to have a girl to talk to. We share all of our secrets, and have become the best of friends.

Friday, May 12, 1871

Mama wasn't feeling well today, so I did the work in her garden. I pulled the weeds, working under the hot sun. I could feel the sweat running down my back, and my bonnet only made me hotter. Luke offered to help me when his work was finished, but mine was nearly finished by then as well. It is a rare day when there is no work to be done, and I appreciated Luke's offer.

Saturday, May 13, 1871

One of our horses has been stolen. Papa believes the outlaws took it. Mama insisted that Papa go after them and make them pay, but Papa refused. He said that it will all come back around someday. Besides, it would be dangerous for Papa to go off after a band of outlaws. Even if some of the boys went with him, it wouldn't be a good idea. Luke wanted to go after them himself, but I know he can't. He's only fifteen. I am more fearful now. Knowing the outlaws were so close to the house while we slept is unsettling. I jump at every sound now. This is going to be a sleepless night for me.

Sunday, May 14, 1871

Mama wasn't feeling well this morning, so I stayed home with her. She had pain in her stomach, and I could see the fear for the baby in her eyes. Never in my life have I

seen anything but stubborn bravery in Mama's eyes. I have always felt I disappointed her by not being headstrong or spirited. I try to make up for it by being helpful and doing what she needs me to do. Mama and I have never been close, but the more time I spend with her, the more I see who she really is.

Monday, May 15, 1871

Mama's pain was much worse this morning. Papa took her into town to see the doctor. The doctor asked her to stay in the hotel for three days so he can watch over her a little better and be sure she's all right. Papa paid for the hotel, and returned home alone. It's strange for Mama to be gone. I have never spent a single night with her away. I miss her very much, and I pray she and the baby will be well.

Tuesday, May 16, 1871

A frightening day. After breakfast, Papa and the boys went out to work in the fields. Danny and Levi stayed with me. Since I had milked the cows early, like I do every morning, I began to clean up after breakfast. Danny played with Levi on the floor, and all was quiet for a little while. I heard horses outside, so I looked out the open door, expecting to see visitors. Instead, I saw three rough-looking men, climbing off their horses and looking around. They each had two guns, and plenty of ammunition from what I could see. I became fearful, realizing I was a young girl alone with two younger boys. I grabbed Papa's rifle from the wall and held it ready. I went to the doorway, with Levi clinging to my skirt. The men greeted me with a stare, and I greeted them by demanding to know what they wanted. My voice told them every bit of the fear I was feeling. Levi became curious and wanted to go see the strange men, but I held him back. One man finally spoke.

"Miss, we don't want any trouble, and no one will get hurt. Just put down your rifle and get us some food," he commanded me.

I waited for a few moments, then decided that feeding them would be the best way to get rid of them. I told them to stay outside while I went into the house with the boys. Setting the rifle against the stove, I gathered our biscuits and bacon from breakfast to give to them. Danny and Levi followed me as I took the food to the men. They accepted the food without gratitude, and ordered me to water their horses. Danny and I led the horses to the well, and I held Levi by the hand. As the horses drank, I watched hopefully for Papa to come across the prairie. But Papa was nowhere to be seen, nor were any of my brothers. How I wished Mama was home at that moment! I took the horses back, expecting the men to leave immediately. I was wrong. One of the men grabbed my wrist and pulled me closer.

"You're a pretty girl," he said, smelling of dirt and smoke. "Why don't you come with us and live a better life. I'd make you a good husband, and you'd never have a house to care for!" He and the other men laughed a harsh, coarse laugh. I had never been more frightened in my life. Danny sent Levi into the house, and looked as if he wanted to fight against the men. I yelled for him to go inside, and he obeyed me. I tried to pull my wrist from the man's tight grip, growing more fearful by the second. One of the other men finally told him to turn me loose, and he did. I ran into the house, grabbed the rifle, and ordered the men off the property. They took their time, and I

stood ready with the rifle until they were out of sight. I sat on the threshold, clutching the rifle and shaking with fear. Danny wrapped his arms around my neck, and Levi began asking a million questions. I didn't answer, so Levi eventually stopped questioning and went into the house to play. Danny sat by my side, trying to comfort me. I couldn't make myself let go of the rifle, and I continued to watch for the men to return. I was still very frightened, and I thanked God that the three of us were safe.

At noon, I saw Papa and the boys walking home in the distance. I suddenly felt like a little girl, wanting only for Papa to hold me and keep me safe. I jumped up and, finally setting down the rifle, I ran toward Papa, beginning to cry. I reached Papa and threw my arms around his neck. Papa was worried and confused, holding me until I could explain. As we walked back to the house, I told him everything that happened. Papa reacted in the expected way. My brothers all thought I was very brave, but Jonah said it might have been fun to marry an outlaw. Papa agreed I had been brave and done the right things. I didn't let Papa out of my sight for the rest of the day; he understood how frightened I had been. As I sit alone in my room, I imagine all of the horrible things that could have happened to me, to my little brothers. I am very grateful everything is all right. I am still a little nervous, and I don't feel much like sleeping.

Wednesday, May 17, 1871

After a sleepless night, I asked Papa if I could go stay with Mama. He agreed, knowing how fearful I am of being home alone while he works the fields. Samuel drove me into town, leaving me at the hotel. I ran up to Mama's room, a bag of my things in my hand. Mama was surprised to see me. I told her what happened yesterday, and she felt terrible she hadn't been there. I assured her everything was fine, and that she shouldn't worry. Mama and I talked for most of the day. The doctor says she can go home tomorrow. I'm glad.

Mama still has a bad feeling about the baby. Sometimes I think Mama knows things, like Danny does. She always seems to know when one of us is hurt, even before we come home. Mama's fear seems to have calmed her a bit; she is much easier to talk to now. Mama told me about her life before she was married, how she lived in a large mansion on a cotton plantation. She wore dresses with large skirts and danced waltzes at parties. I believe she misses her home, and her wealthy life, though she didn't say so. I am staying with Mama tonight, and we'll go home tomorrow morning.

Thursday, May 18, 1871

Mama and I returned home today. Mama is still having a little pain, but not very much. Papa and my brothers were grateful for Mama's return; they can't cook well on their own. Papa told me Sarah came yesterday when I wasn't home. She will probably visit again soon. Or maybe I will go to visit her. I miss her when we don't visit often. If she doesn't come first, I will visit her tomorrow.

Friday, May 19, 1871

I went to visit Sarah. Her house looks very nice now, and the barn does as well. Lyle and Rob came in from working, and we all ate lunch together. Sarah and I then went for a walk, and I asked her why she hasn't been visiting often. I received a surprising and disagreeable answer.

"I've been visiting with James Conner," she said, never once looking shy or nervous. "His family lives on a farm a few miles from here. He's very nice, and I like him very much."

Oh, dear. I don't want to lose my best friend. We just met, and now she'll end up getting married. I am happy for her, and she looks very happy as well, but I still hope that she stays here for a long time.

Saturday, May 20, 1871

Sarah and Rob came today, and the boys decided to have horse races. Sarah and I sat on the fence, with Levi between us and Danny beside me. Mama and Papa had gone into town because Mama wanted to send letters to her family. The horse races wouldn't have been approved of, and I told my brothers so, but that didn't stop them. Samuel didn't race, of course, leaving Luke, Jonah, Micah, and Rob to race. I sat in fear that someone would be hurt, and it soon happened. Rob and Micah were racing against each other. Rob cut in front of Micah, and Micah's horse reared, causing him to fall to the ground. I jumped from the fence and ran into the field where Micah was. Thankfully, Micah was all right, with just a bump on his head. He was on the verge of tears, but held them in bravely. Sarah came into the field, yelling at Rob for not being careful. I was angry with Rob, too, but I kept quiet. I walked with Micah, ignoring Rob as best as I could. Luke and Rob nearly got into a fight, but Sarah and I kept them apart. Sarah thought it best that they leave, not wanting anything else to happen. When Mama and Papa heard the story, they weren't very happy with us. Micah has a great bruise on his forehead. We were told never to race the horses again, and Rob isn't allowed to visit for a while. I'm glad. I don't like him at all.

Monday, May 22, 1871

When I went to milk the cows this morning, I found a calico cat curled up in the hay. Mama said we could keep her because she'll keep rats and other animals out of the barn. We all love her very much already, and she seems to like us, too. At least now there's another female about.

Tuesday, May 23, 1871

I feel very lonesome. Sarah hasn't come to visit, Mama won't allow me to visit her, and my brothers aren't much company. I did my chores, helped Mama cook, and swept the floor. I was sad all day, but I didn't let it show. Perhaps tomorrow will be a better day.

Wednesday, May 24, 1871

Papa went to town today, and came home with a letter from Ben. He says he misses us very much, but he's having a wonderful time. He and Penny are very happy, and Mr. and Mrs. Walker send their regards. I miss Ben so much. He always used to make me laugh, even if I was sad. He kept Luke from bothering me like he always does. Ben was the best older brother I could have had.

Thursday, May 25, 1871

Mama began a new quilt today. I offered to help, but she wouldn't let me. She said it's a quilt she must make by herself. She did allow me to begin my own quilt. I'm using scrap pieces from the clothes Mama has made for us over the years. Each of the pieces is unique and they must fit together in a perfect way. Mama told me it's the same with life. Everything has to fit together in order for things to go smoothly. Sometimes, it seems as though the pieces aren't stitched together correctly, but that is God's job. I trust Him to make the pattern of my life.

Friday, May 26, 1871

This morning, as I went to milk the cows, I saw a rider in the distance. When I entered the barn, I found a handful of wildflowers tied with a ribbon on the milking stool. A small note on top simply said, "For Mary." I wonder who left them there. Was it the rider I saw in the distance? If so, who was it? When Papa came into the barn, he asked me if I knew who the young gentleman was. I told him I didn't. Papa laughed a little, I suppose because his only little girl is growing into a young woman before his very eyes!

Saturday, May 27, 1871

Sarah laughed when I told her of my flowers. She is used to receiving such things from James. But there is a difference: she knows who her suitor is; I do not.

Monday, May 29, 1871

Papa went to town and came home with three letters. One was from Mama's sister Rebecca. I've never met Aunt Rebecca, but she wrote that she is coming to visit Mama. We don't know when she will be here, but Mama is excited, for she hasn't seen her sister in twenty years. The second letter was from Papa's brother, telling him that he has come into a great deal of money, and wants to help in our education. He wants Papa to send the boys to school in Boston, where Uncle Ralph lives. What a troublesome letter; Samuel immediately wanted to go. Papa stared at him for a few minutes, and then told him it was his own decision. Samuel is very happy. He wants an education so badly. I do as well, but I could never leave home. The third letter was from Mama's mother, requesting Mama give up the frontier life and come home. According to her mother, Mama should raise her children in civilized country, not wilderness. My grandmother has a strange way of thinking.

Everyone talked long about Uncle Ralph's offer. Samuel would be satisfied to leave tomorrow. Luke hates school, and argued that he knows all he needs to in order to be a farmer. Papa asked me if I wanted to go, but I could tell he already knew my answer. I replied with a simple no. Jonah didn't want to go, Micah looked afraid to go, and Danny and Levi are too young. Papa wrote a letter back to Uncle Ralph, which Samuel will take into town to mail tomorrow when he goes to find out about his travel route. I have never seen Samuel this animated. He is so happy and excited. I hope he'll be as happy when he is away from home as he is now.

Tuesday, May 30, 1871

Mama and I began mending Samuel's clothes so he will look his best in Boston. He is leaving tomorrow.

Wednesday, May 31, 1871

Samuel left early this morning, looking very nice in his Sunday best. Papa drove him into town after we all said goodbye. Samuel will take a stagecoach to the nearest train station. Mama mourned the loss of her second son, but rejoiced in the fact that he is going to be well educated. Mama wants her sons to have the best, and a good education is the best Samuel could have. Papa returned home with a thoughtful expression; he put away the horse and wagon and went out into the fields. I knew what he was thinking: his two eldest sons are gone, and he still has a farm to run. It will be hard to get on without Ben and Samuel. I miss Samuel already, but I know he is happy. I will try to help Papa more often; only Luke, Jonah, and Micah can help now. Mama would, but she is expecting, and I don't mind working in the fields.

Thursday, June 1, 1871

To celebrate the first day of June, Sarah and I went swimming in the deep part of the creek. We wore only our petticoats and had a wonderful time. We made sure no boys were around, of course. Sarah is a strong swimmer, but I am not. We did manage to have fun. It began to rain, so we pulled on our dresses and ran home. Mama helped me dry off, though my hair is still damp. I am glad I was able to go swimming, and that I have a friend to spend time with.

Friday, June 2, 1871

It was still raining this morning. Papa stood in the doorway after breakfast, looking at the sky. Mama looked out as well, asking what Papa thought. Papa shook his head; the sky is dark and threatening. I fear tornadoes. A tornado could take away everything we own, and our lives as well. I spent the day in prayer as I went about my chores. The animals were restless; they always know when a storm is coming long before it does. I've learned to trust their instincts.

Saturday, June 3, 1871

We are all in the cellar, listening to the storm raging overhead. It struck early this morning. I had just finished milking the cows when Papa and Luke ran into the barn and yelled that a tornado was coming across the fields. We began letting the cows and horses loose; they have a better chance on their own, and we can find them later. I picked up Calico, our cat, and ran with Papa and Luke to the house. I grabbed my diary from my room and hurried down the ladder into the cellar. Mama and the other boys were already there, Luke and Papa followed me. Papa latched the door securely.

Writing by the lantern light helps to calm me. Calico is lying next to me, and Levi is crying with fear in Mama's arms. Papa is sitting next to Mama, comforting her. Luke and Jonah are sitting silently, and Micah is trying to look brave. Danny moved over beside me and picked up Calico, holding her in his lap. The storm is still raging, the wind swirling and blowing loudly. I can hear things moving above us, and I wonder what is going on outside. Are our animals safe? Are the house and barn still standing? I pray the damage is little. It's quieter now; Papa is going outside.

Later—

I have seen destruction without equal. We exited the cellar to find the house still standing. However, both of our windows were devoid of glass, Mama's rocking chair was smashed against the wall, and three of our chairs were broken. We stepped through the broken glass on the floor and went out into the sunshine. Before our eyes, the barn lay in splinters, completely destroyed. Papa looked so sad; he built the barn with his own hands. Eight of the cows stood around the barn, wondering where to go. I don't know what's become of the other two cows. All nine horses (including the foal) were nearby as well, obviously shaken by the storm. Papa and the boys pulled what they could use from the barn. Papa found his tools and went to work repairing the corral for the animals. Mama and I tried to set the house in order. Mama swept the broken glass while I gathered the splintered pieces of the chairs and put them in the woodpile. As we cleaned, Papa came into the house to report that only the corn and wheat and Mama's garden survived. I asked Papa if I could go and make sure that Sarah and her family were safe. Papa agreed, sending Luke with me.

Luke and I arrived on the Hamilton's property to find that everything had been completely destroyed. Sarah and her family were nowhere in sight. Luke realized that they were in the cellar, and that the door was blocked by the fallen house. Luke and I ran to the house and began pulling away the boards. Some of them were very heavy, and it took all of our strength to move them. We finally cleared the debris from the trap door of the cellar and pulled it open. Lyle was the first to climb out, reaching back in for his new baby, born during the storm. He handed the tiny baby girl to me, then helped Nora climb out. Sarah and Rob followed. Nora cradled her

baby, Lily, as everyone saw what had become of their new home. Sarah's hands flew to her mouth as she began to cry. Rob shook his head in disbelief. Lyle looked around, and then said, "At least we still have a cellar." Nora burst into tears, and Lyle placed his arm around her shoulders. Luke suggested I take Nora and Sarah to our house, while he, Rob and Lyle tried to salvage what they could from the property. When Nora, Sarah, and I arrived home, Mama took Lily into her arms and the long conversations began. Luke, Rob, and Lyle arrived soon after, having saved only a few tools, Nora's hairbrush, and a thimble. Our house was full of people, and Mama told the Hamilton's they would stay at our house until further arrangements could be made. The sleeping arrangements are the strangest. My brothers, Rob, Lyle, and Papa are sleeping in the attic. Mama and Nora are sleeping in Mama and Papa's room. Lily is sleeping on the trundle bed, surrounded by pillows and blankets for safety. Sarah and I were going to share my room, but there simply wasn't enough room. Therefore, Sarah is sleeping in my bed, and I am sleeping on the table. I have a blanket and Calico for warmth, and a prayer for a safe night.

Sunday, June 4, 1871

I awoke this morning as Papa was coming out of the attic. Having slept in my dress, I got up and followed him outside. Papa stood at the fence for a moment, and I stood next to him, wondering what he was thinking. Papa took a deep breath and turned to me. He instructed me to choose two of the cows for us to keep, and he would sell the rest to several of the farmers who lost their cows to the storm. After all, we sell the milk we don't need, so we only need two cows anyway. Papa decided we would keep

our horses along with the two cows. They will have to stay in the corral until the barn is rebuilt. Papa took the cows into town to sell. Everyone is meeting in town in order to help each other in any way they can. Several houses and barns on neighboring farms have to be rebuilt. We spent our day clearing the debris from the barn, saving what could be used. Mama and Nora watched and cooked. Sarah and I helped the men clear the barn. It was hard work, but now we are ready to rebuild. First, the Hamiltons' house had to be rebuilt. Until then, they are going to live at our house. I don't mind having other women in the house, and Lyle is very nice, but I'm not enjoying having Rob so close. He isn't the nicest person I've met. He and Luke still don't like each other, and Levi shies away from him. Danny, however, seems to see something in Rob that I don't. Danny doesn't mind being around Rob at all. I don't know how Sarah can stand to live with him; I can't for much longer. Mama is enjoying being a hostess. She is very happy; she misses the social life she once enjoyed. I suppose I'll go to sleep now. I'm tired from the work, and there is more to do tomorrow.

Monday, June 5, 1871

Early this morning, I went to milk our cows. Papa and Lyle soon followed, loading Papa's wagon with lumber. Soon, everyone was heading to the Hamiltons' property to begin working on their house. Micah, Danny, and I stayed behind, having a few chores to do first. We were about to walk to the Hamiltons' house when a wagon approached. The wagon stopped, and a well-dressed woman stepped out. I knew immediately she was my Aunt Rebecca, having the same blond hair, green eyes, and delicate frame Mama has. Her clothes were very fancy, showing her wealth. She looked worn from the trip, but her eyes burned with the

same fire as Mama's. The man took her huge trunk from the wagon and drove away, leaving Aunt Rebecca staring at me and my brothers.

"You must be Mary," she said, resting her small gloved hand on my shoulder. "You look like your father. Goodness me, there are so many boys in your family, I'm not sure which two these boys are!"

I introduced Micah and Danny, and told Aunt Rebecca where everyone else was. She became a bit fearful, I suppose of tornados, and went into the house. Micah and I lugged Aunt Rebecca's trunk into the house and set it in the corner. Aunt Rebecca seemed stunned at the roughness of our house. According to what Mama has told me, Aunt Rebecca is a woman of high society and unprepared for life on the prairie. I told Aunt Rebecca that we were going to the Hamiltons' property to work, and she came with us, none too pleased about having to walk two miles. When we arrived, Mama greeted Aunt Rebecca, and they sat down to talk. Nora was sitting with Lily, and Sarah was helping the men work. I began working, too. Much of the frame of the house was already completed, and there wasn't much for me to do but hand Papa's tools to him. Sarah spent most of the day with James Connor as he helped with the house. I watched them, and I can tell they really like one another. Sarah looks very happy when she is with James. Mama and Aunt Rebecca spent the entire day talking, not lifting a finger to work. Nora and I went alone to my house to cook for everyone. Lily slept quietly while Nora and I prepared a meal for fourteen people. Since there weren't enough chairs left for our table, my brothers and I ate outside. They told me about working on the Hamiltons' house, and we talked quietly about Aunt Rebecca. Micah and I agreed Aunt Rebecca won't stay long, and Danny smiled his agreement. Later, our sleeping arrangements changed once again as Aunt

Rebecca is sleeping in my room, Sarah is sleeping on the table, and I am on the floor. I can tell Aunt Rebecca is very uncomfortable, but so am I.

Tuesday, June 6, 1871

More work on Sarah's house. With everyone working together, it should be done soon. There wasn't much use in me being there, so I stayed home with Mama, Aunt Rebecca, Nora, and Lily. I am helping Mama with her quilt, for she is going to give it to Nora and Lyle, since theirs was lost in the tornado. Nora helped as well, but she doesn't know that it is for her. Surprisingly, Aunt Rebecca doesn't know how to sew. She has never needed to. Instead, she sat and talked to Mama, gossiping about people Mama used to know. Nora and I were ignored, but happy to be. Nora is like me: quiet, thoughtful, and shy. We glanced at each other with disgusted looks as Aunt Rebecca talked. She doesn't seem to know how to keep quiet. In order to avoid having to do this every day, Nora and I sewed as fast as we could, and got a great deal done. My back and fingers are sore, and I'm sleeping on the floor again.

Wednesday, June 7, 1871

This evening, I grew tired of having so many people in the house. I went outside and sat on the fence, petting one of the horses. I just wanted to be alone for a few moments. I thought of so many things: about how much I miss Ben and Samuel, about the flowers on the milking stool, and about how different everything feels. Soon, Papa joined me, sitting beside me and commenting that it was a little too noisy in the house. Papa put his

arm around my shoulders and told me that he knows how I feel. Papa and I are so similar, feeling the same about things oftentimes. I think he understands me better than Mama ever will. Mama tries, but she and I are very different. I sat with Papa until nightfall, and then we went inside. At least the floor is cool in this warm weather.

Later –

Everyone just went back to bed. Aunt Rebecca woke the entire house when she ran screaming from her room. Someone had put a little snake in her bed. It was perfectly harmless, but it scared her very much. I had to pick it up and throw it outside for her. She was reluctant to go back to bed, but finally did. I have a suspicion as to how that snake got there, but I won't say anything. I doubt Aunt Rebecca will be staying with us very much longer.

Thursday, June 8, 1871

Just as I suspected, it was Jonah who put the snake in Aunt Rebecca's bed. Only my brothers and I know, for we think it was a good joke and don't want Jonah to get into trouble. It was harmless, and Luke said it serves her right. I think it's a good laugh.

Friday, June 9, 1871

The Hamiltons' house was completed today, too much rejoicing, but they will still be staying with us for a few more days. Though the house is finished, there is no furniture to fill it. As soon as the beds are made, a stove is purchased, and our quilt is finished, they will move into

their new house. Nora's eyes filled with tears when she saw the completed house. Everyone was very happy, but too tired to celebrate. That can wait until later.

Saturday, June 10, 1871

During breakfast this morning, Papa asked Lyle what pieces of furniture he would need first. Before Lyle could answer, Sarah announced that she wouldn't need a bed, for she is going to marry James. We all sat in stunned silence; no one was expecting her to say that. After the initial shock, everyone began to talk and question at once. Lyle told his sister she should wait, but Sarah wouldn't hear of it. She became very angry and left the table, storming outside. No one followed her, though I wanted to; Papa saw what I was thinking and shook his head slightly. No one has said another word about her all day. Now it's late, and Sarah isn't home. Lyle and Rob are leaving to find her.

Sunday, June 11, 1871

We didn't go to church today. Lyle and Rob were gone for a long time, and returned with news that James is gone as well. We assume that he and Sarah have run off to get married. I can tell Lyle is upset, but I know he's just worried about Sarah. I have prayed for her all day. I pray she is safe and will return soon. God gave me a friend, and now she is gone. However, I pray she and James will be happy. I will miss her.

Monday, June 12, 1871

We received a letter from Samuel. He is enjoying city life. I know he misses us, but I don't think he misses home. He wrote about how beautiful Boston is. I don't believe Boston can compare with our beautiful prairie farm.

Tuesday, June 13, 1871

This morning, the Hamiltons went home. They have beds now, and have purchased a stove as well. Everything else is still being built. Soon everything will be the same as it was.

Wednesday, June 14, 1871

When I went to milk the cows this morning, I found a bundle of wildflowers around the cows' necks. The same note – "For Mary" – accompanied them, and they were lovely. After I finished with the cows, I put the flowers in one of Mama's vases on the table. Aunt Rebecca said they were very romantic. I still don't know who they are from. Papa began working on our barn today. Luke, Jonah, and Micah helped, and Lyle and Rob came to help in the afternoon. Rob pulled my braid when I gave him a drink of water. He teases me often, but I try not to pay him much attention. He often makes himself hard to ignore.

Thursday, June 15, 1871

We've all been working so hard cleaning and rebuilding after the tornado that our fields and gardens

have been ignored. Since Mama and Aunt Rebecca were talking, I went to work in Mama's garden. The weeds were terrible, and it took all day. Now the garden looks nice and healthy again. Papa said he was proud of me.

Friday, June 16, 1871

Aunt Rebecca left today. She told Mama she was sorry, but she "simply could not bear being uncomfortable for another second." Papa and Danny drove her into town, and she took the stagecoach from there. Mama was sad, but my brothers and I were happy to see her leave. Aunt Rebecca doesn't belong on the prairie. It's strange, but Mama seems a little glad that she's gone, too. I think Aunt Rebecca's visit has shown Mama she is no longer a society woman; she is a frontier wife. She's always been one, but she knows it now. Mama smiled at me a little more understandably through the day. I think she learned a few things from Aunt Rebecca's visit.

Saturday, June 17, 1871

I went to town with Papa today. He went to the general store to replace a few tools that were lost in the tornado. Mr. Bailey was very nice, as always. When we returned home, Mama had just finished the quilt. She took it to Lyle and Nora, who were very grateful. There is still no word about Sarah or James, but I'm sure they are fine.

Sunday, June 18, 1871

We all went to church today. Reverend Wilson said a prayer for all of the things lost in the tornado to be restored. He has been helping rebuild things as well. Reverend Wilson is a very nice man, and he is the thread that holds our small community together. After church, Mama began a new quilt. I'm still working on mine.

Monday, June 19, 1871

Our foal is sick. Papa knows all about horses, but he doesn't know what's wrong with the poor little thing. There's been at least one person watching him all day. We're afraid the foal will die if he lies down. I don't want to lose him, but I don't want him to suffer either. Papa is going to let Luke sleep outside to watch him. I pray our foal makes it through the night.

Tuesday, June 20, 1871

As Mama and I cleaned after breakfast this morning, we heard a gunshot. We both looked at each other and knew that Papa had shot the foal. It was for the best; the poor thing was suffering too much. The foal's mother is distraught. I gave her a good brushing, and I think that comforted her. When I went back to the house, I found Mama sitting on her bed crying. I was afraid she was having pains again, but she assured me she was fine. She was crying for our mare. Mama rubbed her stomach and talked about how terrible it would be to lose a child. I could tell she was concerned for her baby. I told her everything would be all right, but I don't think Mama believes it.

Wednesday, June 21, 1871

Papa works on the barn every day. He knows how to do it; he built our first barn. I worked in Mama's garden. It's really looking very lovely. I'm proud of my hard work. Mama lets me wear her broad-brim sun hat because my bonnet is too hot in the sun. Rob and Lyle came to help with the roof of the barn. Nora brought Lily, and sat in the sun with Mama. It was a productive day for everyone.

Thursday, June 22, 1871

Rob came today. He came to show me a letter which they received from Sarah. It simply said that Sarah and James are married, happy, and will be fine. Sarah refuses to come home or tell anyone where she is. I gave the letter back to Rob without a word.

"I know. I miss her, too," he said as he left. I imagine he does miss his younger sister. I miss my brothers, and I hope I don't lose any more. I just realized that, for the first time, Rob was nice to me. I guess he knows how much I miss Sarah, and he knows how it feels. He'll probably be back to himself tomorrow.

Friday, June 23, 1871

I was right about Rob. He teased me all day long when he wasn't helping with the barn. I asked him to leave me alone, but he wouldn't. I know Ben would have defended me, or maybe Samuel would have, but Luke is the only older brother I have left, and he didn't seem to notice.

Saturday, June 24, 1871

The barn is nearly finished. Papa and the boys are very tired. Lyle and Rob are too, and their own barn still needs to be built. I help when I can. Mostly, I help Mama with Levi and the housework. As he works on the barn, I sometimes see Papa take off his hat and look to the fields. I know he's praying God will keep the fields until he can work on them again. Though Papa can't work in the fields, I still work in the garden. It has become my job to keep the garden in good condition. It's a good job, and I do it as best as I can. I hope to have a good harvest by the end of summer.

Sunday, June 25, 1871

We all went to church today. Jonah fell asleep, but neither Mama nor Papa noticed. I could have fallen asleep, too, but I forced myself to stay awake. Sundays are sometimes too long.

Monday, June 26, 1871

Papa says the barn will be finished tomorrow. Finally, our animals will have a place to stay. Papa also put new glass in our windows today. This time, he made the windows with hinges and a latch. Now we can open and close the windows when we want. Mama loves feeling a cool breeze, and so do I. Now, the house won't feel so hot in the summer.

Tuesday, June 27, 1871

Our barn is finally finished. Neighbors provided us with straw for the animals. Our horses and cows are

now settled happily into their new home. Calico has made a nest for herself in the loft of the barn and is quite satisfied. I'm proud of Papa, who looked at the work with satisfaction. My brothers are proud of the work as well. Lyle and Rob asked Papa to help with their barn, and he agreed. Lyle brought his cow and three horses to stay in our barn until his is built. Through the tornado and rebuilding, I've learned that God gives us neighbors to help each other.

Wednesday, June 28, 1871

Work began on the Hamiltons' barn early this morning. Papa and the boys left the cows and horses to me. Danny helped clean the horses' stalls, while I milked the cows on my own. Mama and Nora took care of the cooking, and I helped with Lily. It was a day like all the others. I long for something different to happen.

Thursday, June 29, 1871

I finished my chores in the barn early this morning, so Mama told me I could go with Papa to the Hamiltons' farm. Since everyone is working so hard, the barn is going up fast. Nora let me hold Lily while she did her housework. Nora talked more today than I've ever heard her talk. She talked about where she lived in Illinois before she married Lyle. She talked about her family, and how much she misses them. She even talked about Sarah, which made me sad. I still miss Sarah very much. I wish she would write me a letter. I don't want to know where she is or make her come home. I would just like to hear from her, and know she is safe and sound.

Friday, June 30, 1871

We got a letter from Ben today. The son of the postmaster, Paul, smiled at me sweetly when he brought it. I wonder if he is the one bringing me flowers. Ben wrote that all is well, and he has seen the ocean! He described it, but I still can't imagine so much water. I always wanted to be brave like Ben and see the world, but I just can't do it. For now, I'm satisfied with Ben's detailed letters.

Saturday, July 1, 1871

As I went to milk the cows this morning, I saw dark clouds forming on the horizon. I prayed that another tornado wouldn't come and destroy all of our hard work. The sky looked threatening throughout the day, but the work on the Hamiltons' barn continued. Papa said we can't let a little thing like a storm scare us. I know he's right, but I still feel a bit fearful.

Sunday, July 2, 1871

We went to church today. Reverend Wilson prayed against any storms that would threaten our farms again. I prayed, too. It would be too terrible to face another storm.

Monday, July 3, 1871

The rain poured today, but the weather was very hot. Papa and the others worked on the barn in the rain. I stayed home with Mama, Danny, and Levi. Mama and I quilted for most of the day. My quilt is coming along pretty well, but not very fast. I can't sew as fast as Mama can. Perhaps someday I'll learn all of her skills.

Tuesday, July 4, 1871

Today is Independence Day, but we all stayed home because of the storms. I was only out of the house long enough to milk the cows. I've decided to name our cows Bess and Ann. Mama thinks it's foolish to give names to farm animals, but I love them very much and think they should have names. I'm calling the Hamiltons' cow Sue, but I doubt they will keep that name for her.

Being in the house with my brothers all day was trying. Papa wouldn't allow anyone to go outside in the lightning storm. The thunder was terribly loud, crashing without stop. Luke entertained us with stories, some true and some fantastically imagined. Jonah would be sure to add things if he was a part of the story. As the day wore on and we began to grow weary, we ate an early dinner and went to bed. I've never been in bed this early, and I'm not very sleepy. I've written all I can in my diary for today, so I'll find something else to do.

Wednesday, July 5, 1871

We received a letter from Samuel today. Paul brought it even though it was raining. Samuel wrote that Boston is lovely, he misses us, and that he met a pretty young woman named Patricia. A chance of marriage wasn't mentioned, but I'm sure it will be in a future letter. Samuel has a whole new life now, and I doubt he will ever return to his old life here.

Thursday, July 6, 1871

I grow more grateful for God's protection every day. This morning dawned with blue skies and sunshine. Our work began happily. After we finished our chores at home, we all went to the Hamiltons' farm in hopes of finishing the barn. Everyone worked very hard. At noon, we ate a quick lunch and went back to work. I really had nothing to do, but watched as the men worked. In the afternoon, Nora needed some things from town, and Mama volunteered Danny and me to go get them because, as Mama put it, we weren't being useful. The two of us started off across the prairie, and Rob caught up with us. Nora had sent him to help carry things. I was about to send him back when Danny tugged on my arm and pointed to the sky. A dark cloud loomed on the horizon, but Rob said not to worry, and lifted Danny onto his back. For as much as I dislike Rob, Danny seems to like him. We all walked silently across the prairie.

Before we reached town, a great wind nearly blew us down. The black cloud raced across the sky, bringing a tornado with it. I stood in fear, for there was no shelter to protect us from the storm. I was terrified. Suddenly, Rob grabbed my hand and, still holding Danny, ran across the field to a small ravine. My bonnet flew off as we ran, and I was running hard to keep up with Rob's long steps. There were pieces of things flying through the air, and something sharp hit the side of my face. I barely noticed the pain in our attempt to reach safety. When we reached the ravine, Rob immediately placed Danny on the ground. I pulled off my apron and covered Danny's head. Rob then took his jacket and covered both of our heads. At that moment, I felt very grateful for Rob; there protecting Danny and me. He continued to whisper that we would be all right, and that the storm would pass over us. I prayed ever harder as the wind grew fiercer. As the tornado came closer, we were struck by all sorts of flying debris. I could see Rob's face, and it once clouded with pain as something hit him.

I asked if he was hurt badly, he didn't reply as the storm was too loud to be heard. It seemed to last forever.

Then, just as suddenly as it appeared, the storm ended, leaving us in a welcome silence. Removing the jacket and apron from our heads, we were stunned to see the sun shining as if nothing had happened. Danny put his hand to my face, and I remembered being hit by something. I made sure Danny was all right, and he was, but Rob wasn't as lucky. His leg had been cut very badly by a flying board. He wasn't able to walk, so I told Danny to hurry home and get Papa and Lyle. Danny looked frightened, but went off bravely. I was about to cry, but I didn't want Rob to see my weakness. I instead sat quietly, having wrapped my apron around Rob's leg to stop the bleeding. Rob thanked me, apologizing for ruining my apron. He was very different then, not as arrogant as I've seen him before. It was as though he was grateful for life itself. I thanked him for protecting Danny and me, but he said it was nothing. "Anyone would have done the same thing," he told me. Never once did he look into my eyes. He did, however, take the sleeve of his jacket and stop the blood that was running down the side of my face. It was very nice of him. Silence followed, and he seemed just as shy as me. Soon after that, Danny arrived with Papa and Lyle. Papa hugged me close, happy to see I was safe. He then looked to Rob, who was already leaning on Lyle's arm. Papa took Rob's other arm, and we all climbed out of the ravine. Danny held my hand all the way home. We went to the Hamiltons' house, because everyone was still there. Mama held me tightly as she cried, saying, "I never should have sent you out there." It wasn't her fault, though. She bandaged my face, and I tried very hard not to cry from the pain. Rob had his leg cleaned and properly bandaged, and Mama found out that I had ruined my apron and lost my bonnet. She wasn't angry, but happy that they were the only things lost. Luckily, this tornado brought no damage. After my family and I returned home, we said a prayer of thanksgiving to God for saving our property, and our lives. As I lie in bed, I am very grateful for God's blessings. I also think Rob isn't as bad as I thought him to be.

Friday, July 7, 1871

Thankfully, the sky was blue this morning, and no clouds blackened the sky. I talked to the cows as I milked them and told them all about my adventure yesterday. They seemed to enjoy the story; I can tell the cows anything. Mama bandaged the cut on my face again. I decided to check on Rob since Papa was going to help finish the barn anyway. Rob told the story to my brothers again, and he told it as though he was a hero. I stared at him, not understanding how he could have changed so since yesterday. Rob seemed to see the look in my eyes, for he stared back and looked sorry. He told the boys I had been very brave as well, but I don't think they believed him. I felt bad, but I didn't want Rob to think I did.

Papa and the others worked late to finish the barn. Tomorrow the animals will be moved to their new home. I'm glad the barn is finished; now Papa can focus on the crops.

Saturday, July 8, 1871

I milked Sue for the last time this morning. Lyle came to get her and the horses before I was finished. I told Lyle I had named her, and he said it was a fine name. I'm glad that she'll still be called Sue, but I'm sure she'll miss Ann and Bess.

Papa worked in the fields today, having neglected them for weeks. He came home having found that the wheat is diseased. He was so disappointed. The wheat will have to be plowed down and replanted, and we can only hope to have a decent crop now. Papa now has to do so much more work than he expected. He will need a lot of help since Ben and Samuel are gone. I suppose I can help Papa in the fields when I'm not working in the garden. I pray our crops will be all right.

Sunday, July 9, 1871

After church today, Papa went out to the wheat field. Mama sent me to get him for dinner. When I found Papa, he was on his knees in the middle of the field, his hat in his hands, praying. I didn't want to disturb him, but I knelt down beside him and began to pray for the wheat as well. After a few minutes, Papa put his hand on my shoulder. The look in his eyes told me everything will be fine. We walked home, and I felt better knowing that Papa's faith in God is strong.

Monday, July 10, 1871

At breakfast this morning we all joined hands to pray. Papa prayed for the meal, then said a different prayer.

"Lord," he began, "You are the true owner of our crops, and You know what is wrong with it. I pray You clean our wheat, and we thank You for it. Amen."

Mama looked questioningly at Papa, but, as we began our meal, something amazing happened. A loud crash of thunder startled us from the table. When we reached the door, everyone took a deep breath. A great black cloud hovered over our wheat fields, pouring rain down onto the wheat. There were no clouds or rain anywhere else; it covered only the wheat.

"It's a miracle," Micah said in amazement. "Just like Papa prayed for."

We watched as the rain continued to pour. Mama told us all to finish our breakfast, and we reluctantly returned to the table. As we ate, we listened to what was happening outside. Just as we finished eating, a second crash of thunder brought us all back to the door. The rain had stopped, and the cloud was gone. We all walked into the field, struggling to make sense of what had just happened. Papa began to look at the wheat, examining it and asking what Luke thought. Luke didn't understand it, but Papa did. The wheat is perfect, even healthier than it had been. Papa laughed with joy, picking Mama up and swinging her around. We were all as happy as could be, and joined hands right there in the field to thank God for the wonderful miracle He gave us. I've never seen anything like it in my life!

Tuesday, July 11, 1871

Papa began work early this morning, while I was still milking the cows. He was in a very happy mood, whistling as he gathered his tools for work. I worked in Mama's garden, almost finishing before the sun became too hot. Now that the weather is truly warm, I imagine all of the fun Sarah and I would have had if she were here. I wonder where she is. I miss her.

Wednesday, July 12, 1871

Papa and Jonah went into town today. When they returned, Jonah's eyes were wide and he nearly burst, telling us a tale of wild horses. Papa explained that about a dozen wild mustangs were brought into town for sale, all of them unbroken. My brothers wanted to go and see them, even Levi. Mama looked doubtful, but Papa approved. Mama sent me along to look after Levi and Danny, and make sure they would be safe. I was happy to go; horses are one of my favorite things. We all followed Jonah to the edge of town where a large corral was set up. The most beautiful horses I have ever seen were contained in that corral. Many men were crowded around, watching as the horses were being ridden. The horses were actually throwing every rider. Though the men were being tossed about, it was the horses who endured the suffering. The men were terribly cruel to them. I couldn't bear to watch it, and I didn't want Danny and Levi to watch either, so I took them home. Micah followed as well, but Luke and Jonah stayed to watch. It's sad to see beautiful wild animals forced to carry a man or pull a plow. We have enough horses without having to break the wild ones. I'll never forget how sad and angry the horses' eyes looked.

Thursday, July 13, 1871

I received two gifts when I milked the cows this morning. The first was another bundle of flowers. The note, however, had changed. This time, it said, "For Mary, With Love." I tucked the note into my apron pocket. The flowers were beautiful, tied with a red ribbon. Who could be responsible for these gifts?

My second gift came from Calico. She brought me a big, fat rat that she had killed. She laid it at my feet

and waited for my approval. I quickly rubbed her head, telling her how very proud I was. She was satisfied, so she took the rat away. I finished milking the cows, and carried Calico and my flowers into the house. Mama gave a dish of cream to Calico and a vase of water to me. My flowers sit on the table, and my note rests inside my diary along with the other two. Perhaps someday I'll know who wrote the notes and gave me the flowers.

Friday, July 14, 1871
Mama sent me with a loaf of bread for Nora today. I was able to hold Lily while Nora did a few things. Rob came in while I was there, and commented that my face looked nearly healed. His leg is better, but not completely. I asked him if it hurt, but he said it didn't. Nora said that Rob is brave, just like his brother. Nora never fails to state the good things about Lyle, and Lyle never fails to tell how much he loves Nora. I hope to have a love like that one day.

Saturday, July 15, 1871
The weather is hot and the mosquitoes are thick. They are everywhere. We are forced to keep the windows open because of the heat. The mosquitoes are everywhere I go, and I can't get rid of them. Levi cries from the bites. At night, I sleep only in my petticoat because of the heat, with a thin sheet over me to keep the mosquitoes away. It's very uncomfortable, but it works. I'm afraid of the fever the mosquitoes bring. However, I know God will protect us.

Sunday, July 16, 1871

During church, poor Reverend Wilson had to slap at mosquitoes while delivering his sermon. In fact, the entire congregation fought to keep the mosquitoes away. At the end of the sermon, Reverend Wilson laughed and said we should pray for God to keep His little creatures at a distance. I think it's a good prayer.

Monday, July 17, 1871

Such a surprise today. I received a letter from Sarah. She wrote that she is happy with James, but she misses everyone. She wrote for me to tell Lyle that she is sorry and he is a wonderful brother. She also wrote for me to tell Rob to behave, and follow his heart. I delivered the messages. Lyle was happy to hear that Sarah is all right. Rob didn't say anything, but his eyes showed a strange mixture of happiness and shyness. The rest of Sarah's letter was vague; she seems lonesome, yet happy.

Tuesday, July 18, 1871

Mama finished my new bonnet today. It's very nice. She is now sewing new things for the baby. I have sadly neglected my quilt. I've been too busy with the garden. Mama doesn't mind. She says sewing can wait until winter.

Wednesday, July 19, 1871

Levi has a fever. I fear it has come from the mosquitoes. He lies very still on the trundle bed, sweating and shivering in his fevered sleep. Mama is sitting by him,

worrying and keeping cool rags on his head. We are all very worried.

Thursday, July 20, 1871

I awoke this morning to find that Jonah and Micah now have the fever as well. Mama had already sent Papa, Luke, and Danny outside; she doesn't want everyone to get sick. She won't let me help her, either. I went out into the morning dew to find Luke and Danny. Papa was already in the fields, though it was beginning to rain. I milked the cows, and Danny helped a little. The four of us ended up spending the day in the barn. The warm rain prevented any work, and Mama kept us out of the house. We worried over my sick brothers, and prayed for their recovery. We talked about the crops, Ben, Samuel, and my flowers. Papa said it won't be long before I know who is giving flowers to me. Whoever it is shouldn't be as shy as I am.

Saturday, August 5, 1871

I have no memory of the events since my last entry. It seems that I, too, fell ill with the fever, and just this morning woke from it. I awoke to Mama's beautiful face, worn with weariness. She gave me some water and held me close. I asked her to explain everything, but she shook her head. She said I must rest and get well. Later, she brought me a bowl of hot broth. Now, I'm in my room alone and under strict orders to keep the door closed. I write slowly and with an aching head. I wonder about my family. Are my brothers well? Is Papa well? I can't think any longer. I must sleep.

Sunday, August 6, 1871

After a long restful sleep, I awoke this morning feeling much better. However, Mama forbade me to leave my bed. I asked about Papa and the boys, but Mama avoided my questions. I've been alone in my room all day. When Mama brings something for me to eat, I try to see out the door, but I never can. I'm worried. I think Mama is hiding a horrible truth from me.

Monday, August 7, 1871

Another day of confinement to bed. This morning, Mama brought a surprise with breakfast. She brought me a book that she had planned on giving me for Christmas, but thought I could use now. It's called *Little Women*, and it's about four sisters. I've already read eight chapters today, and it's wonderful. Their world is so much different than mine. Now I have other girls to spend time with. I think Miss Alcott is wonderful!

Tuesday, August 8, 1871

When Mama brought my breakfast this morning, I pleaded with her, telling her how well I am. I begged to know if Papa and the boys are well. Mama sat down on my bed, and I noticed how tired and sad she looked.

"It's been such a long illness," Mama began. "Your Papa is still ill, but is beginning to get better. Luke and Danny were hardly sick at all, and are well now. Micah is beginning to come around, but Jonah is still deep in fever. Levi…oh, my baby Levi!"

Mama could hardly bring herself to tell me that the fever has taken Levi from us. Mama and I sat together

and cried until we heard Micah calling. Mama wiped her tears and told me to stay in bed until tomorrow. I sat all day and thought about my dear baby brother. It's unimaginable that he is gone. I do, however, know that he is in heaven with God. I still mourn for him.

Wednesday, August 9, 1871

This morning, Mama asked me to milk the cows. It was her way of allowing me to leave my bed. I dressed eagerly, and realized how weak I really felt. Nevertheless, it felt wonderful to open the door to my room. I saw that Mama had made beds for my brothers on the floor. She couldn't care for them by climbing the ladder to the attic. Mama quickly pushed me out the door while I took one look at Jonah and Micah. Mama closed the door behind me, and I made my way to the barn. The cows greeted me warmly, and I went to work cheerfully. It was wonderful to be outside, to be working, simply to be alive. I sat in the barn with Calico for a long time, holding her in my lap. After a little while, Danny and Luke found me. Danny ran to me and wrapped his arms around my neck. His smile told me more than words ever could. To my surprise, Luke also hugged me tight. I think that he's realized how very important his family is to him. Having a sibling die has brought us all a little closer to one another. I pray that Micah, Jonah, and Papa recover. I also pray for Mama. She needs rest.

Thursday, August 10, 1871

When I awoke this morning, I quickly dressed and determined to help Mama. I found her asleep in her rocking chair. I didn't want to wake her, so I asked Luke to milk the cows for me while I made breakfast. Mama woke up and looked as though she was going to scold me, but she didn't. She instead thanked me and saw to Micah and Jonah. Micah seems well, but Mama is keeping him in bed. Jonah is still very ill. Papa is feeling much better, but Mama advised him to stay in bed until tomorrow. I helped Mama all day, and she was able to rest a little. I'm growing stronger, and I'm grateful.

Friday, August 11, 1871

Jonah's fever broke today, and Micah and Papa were allowed out of bed. I looked after Jonah for most of the day. He is still weak, but his joking is as strong as ever. I know nothing can ever cause Jonah to be down for long. Papa was out in the fields immediately, though he was still too weak to work for long. I'm very thankful the fever is gone. I only wish it hadn't taken Levi with it.

Saturday, August 12, 1871

Jonah insisted upon leaving bed today, and he seems very healthy. Mama proceeded to clean the entire house, hoping to prevent the fever from returning. I helped, for Mama's stomach is too large for her to do some things. She grows more excited daily about the new baby, although I know she still mourns for her lost baby.

Sunday, August 13, 1871

We didn't go to church today. We were all too tired. Lyle and Rob came to see if we were all right, and

were pleased to find that we have recovered. They already knew of Levi's death. I was pleased to see them both, though I felt strangely shy around Rob. I don't know why, but I'm finding him more often in my thoughts.

Monday, August 14, 1871

Today, Mama took my hand and asked me to walk with her. I agreed, and we walked to the small cluster of trees on our property. There, in the shade, was Levi's grave. I saw it for the first time, and it brought tears to my eyes. I miss my dear little Levi. Mama and I sat in the grass beneath the trees, and we talked. We talked for endless hours like the best of friends. It was wonderful, and I love Mama more now than I ever have. Sometimes I feel that Mama is different than she used to be. She's more of a friend.

Tuesday, August 15, 1871

Last night, I dreamed about Rob. I don't remember much of the dream, just that he was there and I was happy. He was in my thoughts the entire day. I worked in the garden to avoid questions about the blush that I'm sure covered my face. I regard Rob in a new light now. I don't dislike him as much as I thought I did. I suppose I have too many idle thoughts.

Wednesday, August 16, 1871

Paul brought two letters today, one from Ben and one from Samuel. Paul is a sweet boy and always brings our letters as soon as he can. Ben wrote about his travels with Penny, and about the baby that they are expecting. I can't think of Ben being a father, though he will make a very good one. Samuel wrote that he is coming home to visit with his soon-to-be bride, Miss Patricia Whitlow. He wants Papa and Mama to approve of her. It should be an interesting visit. City folks and farms don't combine well.

Thursday, August 17, 1871

Papa and the boys have been working hard, preparing to bring in the crops. Mama and I have been working in the house, cleaning and preparing for the harvest of the garden. We will have canning and preserving to do. When we take a break, we work on our quilts. Mama told me the quilt she is making will be mine when I am married. I smiled, and Mama said I could be married before I know it. I really don't know about that.

Friday, August 18, 1871

Mama eagerly awaits Samuel's visit. Since our house is small, Samuel will have to sleep in his old place in the attic. I will sleep on the table while Patricia sleeps in my room. Mama is pleased that Samuel is coming home. I would be more pleased if it were Ben who was returning home.

Saturday, August 19, 1871

I have fully regained my strength. I feel very well now. I thank God for His many blessings. My life is so good because of God's presence in it.

Sunday, August 20, 1871

At church this morning, Reverend Wilson told us he was thankful our family is well and suffered no more losses. He is a very nice man. It's good to know he prays for us. Everyone should do the same and pray for each other.

Monday, August 21, 1871

Samuel and Patricia arrived today. Samuel looks so different. His clothes are very fine, and he looks exactly like I imagine a city man would. Patricia was a sight. She looked even wealthier than Aunt Rebecca did. Her clothes are beautiful, though too elaborate. Her shoes, gloves, parasol, and hat matched her dress, and her brown hair was arranged to frame her face perfectly. She's very dainty, and has fine airs. She greeted everyone with a large smile, her brown eyes shining. She is a pretty girl, but she puts on too many airs. I think she believes herself to be better than us. My brothers and I stood quietly, not knowing what to say. It was dinner time, so Mama played hostess while everyone ate. I'm not sure if Patricia was able to eat anything; she spent the entire meal talking. She told about her family, her schooling, her wealth, and anything else that came into her mind. She also asked numerous questions, most of which were directed to Papa. Papa is a man of few words, and even fewer around strangers. Patricia once asked Papa if he has a favorite child. I immediately saw a twinkle in Papa's eye, and he answered, "Mary is my favorite daughter." Patricia took a few moments before she understood that I am the only daughter. After dinner, I began to clear things away, but Mama told me it could wait until later. I knew she and Papa wanted to talk to Samuel and Patricia alone.

My brothers and I went into the barn and sat. Luke looked at me, and I at him, and we began to laugh. Luke said he couldn't believe the change in Samuel and the absurdity of Patricia. Jonah agreed, and Micah simply said they are both silly. Danny didn't have an opinion, just a smile that showed his agreement. We all agreed that Samuel isn't the same brother that we knew, but he's still our brother. We will be happy for him. I warned Jonah not to put a snake in Patricia's bed, and he reluctantly agreed. When it got dark outside, Papa came to get us. He picked up Danny, who had fallen asleep in the hay, and we all went into the house. I found Mama cleaning the dinner things while Patricia watched and continued to talk. I offered to show Patricia to her room, my room rather, and she was a little taken aback by the bed. I'm sure she sleeps in grander and softer places. However, she smiled and, after kissing Samuel, went to bed without another word. My brothers also went to bed, and Mama and I finished cleaning. Mama giggled and said she is now very happy that she is no longer a society woman. I'm happy, too. We don't need two women like Patricia in one family.

Tuesday, August 22, 1871

I awoke first this morning, so I was very quiet as I went to milk the cows. When I arrived, I found a bundle of flowers on the milking stool. This time, the note read, "Mary, I'm very thankful that you are well." More than ever I long to know who is leaving these gifts. Sometimes, I think it could be Paul, because he smiles at me so sweetly when he comes. Perhaps it's one of the other boys who live on a neighboring farm; there are several boys my age or a little older. Maybe I'll never know who it is. Maybe they are a joke.

Patricia thought they were very sweet. She proceeded to talk about courtship in Boston, and I think it's very stuffy and dull. There are too many rules. I prefer the way things are here. I would have told Patricia what I thought if she had ever stopped talking. Samuel is such a quiet person; why did he choose a girl like Patricia?

Wednesday, August 23, 1871

Even though visitors are here, work must continue. Papa and Luke work in the fields; Luke has overcome his laziness. Jonah, Micah, and Danny help as well. I work in the barn or the house, depending on what is needed. Samuel and Patricia spend all of their time together, and I think they are truly in love. Mama and I work for most of the day, though Mama must sit down sometimes. In over one month, I will have a new brother or sister. I still hope and pray for a sister. It's strange that Mama is still having children while her children are marrying and having children of their own. Mama looks very young, as does Papa. Life works in strange ways.

Thursday, August 24, 1871

As Papa and the boys headed into the fields this morning, Papa asked me to do a favor for him. Since the Hamiltons weren't able to plant crops this year, Papa is going to ask Lyle and Rob to help harvest in exchange for some of the crop and profit. I agreed with the plan and set off for the Hamiltons' farm. When I arrived, Nora greeted me warmly and let me hold Lily. I told her Papa's plan, and she jumped with excitement. She hurried to the door and called for Lyle and Rob, who were in the barn. Nora shouted the news before they even arrived. Lyle was very happy, and thanked me. When Rob came in, I grew very nervous and looked down at Lily to avoid his gaze. However, I couldn't keep my eyes from finding Rob's face. I was surprised to see a blush on his face. Maybe he's been thinking of me as I've been thinking of him.

Rob and Lyle immediately set off for our farm. I stayed with Nora as she gathered a few things for the day. We enjoyed a productive day, and the Hamiltons were able to meet Patricia. I don't think they were very impressed. We have no use for the finery Patricia has. I'm content just as I am.

Friday, August 25, 1871

Last night, I listened as Patricia tossed restlessly throughout the night. She looked tired this morning, but talked cheerfully. She never runs out of things to talk about. I can't even have one conversation without running out of things to say. I'm not as smart as Patricia is. She also has a nice voice, whereas my voice is small and whispery. I never raise my voice, and I rarely talk to people I don't know and trust. Perhaps I should become more like Patricia. I'd like to think I'm all right just being myself.

Saturday, August 26, 1871

The wheat is being harvested. I watch Lily while Nora and Mama do other things. Patricia entertains them with stories of her life and Boston. Samuel goes into the field, but he doesn't help anymore.

To escape Patricia's voice, which I've come to find annoying, I take Lily into the barn and sit in the hay. She likes Calico, and laughs when the horses make a sound. She's a good baby. I only wish Sarah were here to spend this time with me.

Sunday, August 27, 1871

We all went to church today. Patricia dressed in her finest, as did Samuel. They looked very out of place. They are leaving tomorrow. I'm glad.

Monday, August 28, 1871

Samuel and Patricia left today. I think we were all glad to see them leave. Samuel isn't the same person anymore. He's changed so much. As soon as they left the property, Mama sat down in her rocking chair and blew out her breath. She laughed a little as Papa put his hand on her shoulder. Neither expected one of their children to become a city man. Mama said that she has fully released her former life, and never would exchange what she has now to have it back.

Tuesday, August 29, 1871

Work in the fields continues. I milked the cows early, and spent the rest of the day helping Mama with other things. Every day seems the same sometimes.

Wednesday, August 30, 1871

This morning, Danny brought a handful of flowers tied with a ribbon before I went to milk the cows. The note read, "For Mary, the sweetest girl I know." I immediately asked Danny if he was the one who had been giving me these gifts. He shook his head, and I asked if he knew who it was. He nodded, and I asked him who it was, but he only smiled. I suppose I'll never get Danny to say a word about anything. One thing is true: Danny will always keep a secret. But I still have a problem. Who is giving me beautiful flowers, pretty ribbons, and sweet notes?

Thursday, August 31, 1871

I received another letter from Sarah. I miss her so much. She wrote that she misses home and everyone here. She and James are happy, and are faring well in their new home. She still won't tell where they are. I wish she would come home.

Friday, September 1, 1871

We began to gather some of the corn today. I worked in the field with everyone all day. As I worked, I thought about all that had been happening lately. When I spotted Rob coming through the corn, I grew very shy. I set down my basket and hurried through the field to escape. I tried to hurry, still watching for Rob so he wouldn't see me. I lost sight of him, but was still looking over my shoulder. That's when I turned a corner and ran directly into Rob. I hit him so hard I fell down. I was on my side in a dazed silence. Rob looked at me and smiled. He offered his hand and helped me off the ground. I thanked him, but he held my hand for a few more seconds. I felt my heart flutter. He released my hand and told me to be careful next time. I went back to work, but thought about it for the rest of the day. It was a strange new feeling, but I think that it was a good feeling.

Saturday, September 2, 1871

Mama grows more excited about her baby daily. I believe her feeling of dread is gone. At odd moments of the day, she rests her hands on her large stomach, closes her eyes and smiles. I'm excited as well.

Sunday, September 3, 1871

We went to church today. It was rather boring.

Monday, September 4, 1871

Due to pouring rain and lightning, no one worked in the fields today. I felt relieved to be away from Rob. Mama sat in her rocking chair and worked on her quilt. Midway through the day, I asked Mama what the new baby would be named. She looked at Papa and said, "I suppose we should decide on a name." When Ben was born, Mama and Papa agreed to use only Biblical names for their children. Papa pulled the family Bible from the trunk and began to look through it. It passed from hand to hand, and everyone made a suggestion. We began with boy's names, and it was quite a discussion. Peter, Amos, James, Moses, Elijah, and Jeremiah were all suggested before Mama and Papa agreed upon Joseph. Then, they tried to find a girl's name. There are fewer female names in the Bible. Mama and Papa quickly agreed upon Elizabeth. Jonah wanted to use Zipporah, but only because his favorite story is that of Moses. My favorite is Esther's story. I wish I could be as brave as she was. Soon, Mama's baby will arrive, and we'll welcome either Joseph or Elizabeth to the family.

Tuesday, September 5, 1871

Though it was still raining a little, Papa went back to work in the fields. My brothers, Lyle, and Rob went to work as well. Nora stayed home with Lily, so Mama and I spent the day together. I enjoy being with Mama, and she is my best friend. I thought about telling her what I had been feeling about Rob, but I grew so nervous thinking about it that I couldn't say a word. Perhaps one day I will.

Wednesday, September 6, 1871

Papa went to town today, and returned with four laying hens. Mama was pleased, for now she will have eggs whenever she wants them. Papa built a pen for them in the barn, and they seem to like it. Danny is in charge of feeding them, and he seems to enjoy it. He's good with any sort of animal. I guess it's his gentle nature.

Thursday, September 7, 1871

This morning, after milking the cows, I gathered four white eggs from the hens' nests. Mama was pleased to have them. She sent me with two for Nora and a message that she is welcome to have eggs when she needs them. Nora was grateful, and I was nervous, for I felt Rob's gaze as I spoke. I felt so nervous I could hardly finish my sentence. I went home quickly, and went to work in the garden without a word to anyone. I think of Rob so often, but I'm not sure why. Could it be that I'm beginning to like him more?

Friday, September 8, 1871

Paul brought a letter from Ben today. He also handed me a small flower when no one was looking. It made me believe he is responsible for my flowers.

Ben wrote that he misses everyone, but is very happy. I miss him so much. I wish to see him again someday.

Saturday, September 9, 1871

Papa and the boys went into the fields to work early this morning. I expected to see Lyle and Rob, but they never came. By mid-morning, Mama sent me to see if all was well. I didn't want to go, but I did. When I reached the Hamiltons' house, no one was about. I knocked on the door and waited, but all I could hear was Lily's cries. After a few moments, I feared that something was terribly wrong. I opened the door and stepped inside. Lily lay in her crib crying, so I quickly picked her up and held her close. I heard a soft moan, and looked to see Lyle and Nora in bed, ill with fever. Fearing for their lives, I took Lily and ran home. I told Mama and Papa, who had come in from the fields. They hurried off, telling me to stay with Lily. I gave her a little milk, and rocked her to sleep in my arms, worrying about her family. Nora and Lyle are such wonderful people, and I couldn't bear to see them die. I worried about Rob as well. I hadn't seen him, but thought he was probably in the attic, just as ill. When my brothers came in for lunch, I told them all that had happened. I let Micah hold Lily while I fixed what I could for them to eat. By nightfall, Papa returned and said the whole family was sick with fever, and that Mama wanted me to come and help her. Papa walked with me to the Hamiltons' house. I took little Lily with me, for she needed to be cared for. I found Mama caring diligently for the others. Rob had

been in the attic, but managed to climb down with Papa's help to a bed Mama made on the floor. Since all are in a fitful sleep, I am scrawling a few words in my diary. Mama is resting in the rocking chair while I keep watch. Lily is asleep, and has no signs of the fever. I pray she remains well. I will spend the remainder of my watch in prayer.

Monday, September 18, 1871

For over a week we have cared for the Hamiltons, and I have been too weary to write. Nora is well enough to sit in her rocking chair and hold Lily. We are all grateful the fever didn't touch Lily. Lyle is on the mend, but Rob still has a fever. I pray he is well soon.

Tuesday, September 19, 1871

When I knelt down to put a cool rag on Rob's forehead, he took my hand in his. I was frightened by the movement, for he hadn't been awake for days. However, I looked deep in his eyes, and my heart felt like a butterfly. He held my hand tightly and whispered, "Thank you." I smiled, and he held my hand to his chest. Mama was there by then, but she didn't seem to see what passed between Rob and me. Throughout the day, I would catch Rob staring at me, but I didn't feel as shy as before. Instead, I would look back at him and smile. He would smile as well.

Nora convinced Mama and me to go home and rest, thanking us for all we had done. We will check on them again tomorrow. It's good to be home.

Wednesday, September 20, 1871

After our morning chores, Mama and I went back to the Hamiltons' house. Mama walks slowly because her stomach is so large. She will deliver soon. As we walked, I thought of Rob and began to grow very shy. By the time we reached the house, I was too shy to look at Rob. I knew he was looking at me, and I felt myself blushing.

Nora assured us she was well. Lyle is nearly well, also, as is Rob. Mama and I didn't stay long today. As I lie in bed, I wonder about what I feel. It's strange.

Thursday, September 21, 1871

When I went into the barn this morning, I found Calico trying to get into the chicken pen. I quickly pulled her away as the chickens cackled their disapproval. I scolded Calico, and I think she listened. Mama is enjoying having eggs when she needs them. I really don't like eggs at all, so I never eat them.

Friday, September 22, 1871

Lyle and Rob returned to working in the fields today. They worked a little slower than before, but Papa didn't mind. He's very considerate. Nora came and sat with Mama and me. Her cheeks are rosy again. Lily is as healthy as ever, having never caught the fever. We thank God for that.

Saturday, September 23, 1871

Mama, Nora, and I cleared much of the garden today. I pulled the vegetables from the garden while Mama and Nora canned and put them in the cellar. I worked hard in the hot sun, with Mama's sun hat as my only shade. After all of the vegetables were out of the garden, I pulled all of the green stalks from the ground. Once they are dry, Papa will burn them. Soon, all of the neighbors will gather for the harvest celebration. It is one of my favorite times of the year.

Sunday, September 24, 1871

After church today, the doctor asked Mama how she was feeling. Mama is in good spirits and feeling well. I'm eager for the new baby to be born.

Monday, September 25, 1871

This evening, as we all sat together, Mama placed her hands on her stomach and said, "Yes, I believe we will have another son." She smiled, pleased at the thought. Papa said it would be nice to have another daughter, but was sure Mama is right. I hope she's wrong.

Tuesday, September 26, 1871

Papa needed me to work in the corn fields today. Corn stalks always make me itch so much. I can hardly stand it. I long for a bath, but I must wait until Saturday. At least my brothers can go swimming and feel clean. If Sarah were here, so could I.

Wednesday, September 27, 1871

Another day of harvesting corn. We all worked very hard. I saw Rob today, and he smiled at me. I smiled too, but very shyly. I'm slowly overcoming my shyness, and I pray God will help me.

Thursday, September 28, 1871

The harvest continues. My back and arms ache so that I can hardly bear it. Everyone is tired. Mama is working as well, but not as hard. She must save her strength for the birth. My hands are tired, and it's hard for me to write. However, my diary has become my best friend. I can write anything here. I tell Mama most things, but I'm just too shy to tell her about Rob. I can't possibly tell my brothers, and I don't think Papa wants to hear of his only daughter thinking of a young man. It's strange to be unable to tell someone. It's almost as though I have a secret, one that only I know. Perhaps Rob knows as well.

Friday, September 29, 1871

This morning, I found more flowers on the milking stool. This time, they were tied with a sky blue ribbon. The flowers were a little dry and brown on the edges, but they were very special to me. The note read, "Dearest Mary, you grow closer to my heart every day." I blushed when I read it. Papa came into the barn, saw my face and the gifts, and simply questioned, "More flowers?" I just smiled. I feel happy when I receive these gifts, but I would be happier if I knew who they are from.

Saturday, September 30, 1871

We pulled the rest of the corn from the field today. Every time I saw Rob, he smiled at me. I find myself looking for his smile. When he smiles, it's as though I see myself in his eyes, and my heart flutters. After our day of rest tomorrow, we will have to shuck the corn. I don't mind. It's not very hard, and I'll be able to sit down for the day.

Sunday, October 1, 1871

Mama and I stayed home while the others went to church. She doesn't want to leave the house. She's afraid of being away from home when the baby is born. She still believes the baby will be a boy. I still pray for a girl.

Monday, October 2, 1871

We began shucking corn today. We only shuck a portion of the crop, keeping the rest for Papa to sell along with a portion of the wheat. It was refreshing to be able to sit down for the day with my brothers and friends. I enjoy being with the people I love, even if it is while working.

Tuesday, October 3, 1871

Mama grows impatient for the baby to be born. She is eagerly awaiting the moment. I hope she will deliver easily when the time comes. After all of the trouble that Mama has had while expecting, I hope and pray the birth will be very easy.

Wednesday, October 4, 1871

Mama had the baby today! Early this morning, Mama wasn't feeling well, and sent all of the boys outside. I helped her to bed as she cheerfully told Papa to go for Mrs. Davis, the midwife. Mama was so pleased it took time before the pain began to bother her. I was afraid that Mrs. Davis wouldn't arrive in time. However, she came quickly, as large as she is, and went to work. She ordered Papa from the house and forbade him to re-enter. I did everything Mrs. Davis asked then she ordered me from the house as well. I went outside where I found Papa waiting anxiously, while my brothers were working as though nothing unusual were happening. When the Hamiltons arrived, we told them what was happening. Lyle and Rob went to work, and Nora sat with me. I sat in the grass, watching Papa as he paced back and forth. This is his ninth child; he should be used to this wait. Finally, late in the afternoon, a baby's cries pierced the silence of the prairie. Nora and I looked at one another, and Papa stared expectantly at the house. I quietly said one last prayer for a sister. Mrs. Davis opened the door. A smile covered her round face as she said, "David, you can see Jane and your new son now." Papa shouted for joy and hurried into the house. My heart was too happy to consider being sad about another brother. Papa allowed me to go in as well. Little Joseph is a picture of health. Mama held him close, allowing Papa to hold him as well. I hurried to tell the boys of the birth. All the boys were all happy to have another brother. Lyle said I am sadly outnumbered by all these boys. I'm afraid I am, but Joseph is so sweet that I won't hold it against him.

Thursday, October 5, 1871

After a restful night, Mama returned to her duties, though she didn't work as hard as usual. Papa told her to stay in bed, but Mama's happy spirit wouldn't allow it. I held Joseph while she made breakfast. Danny stood beside me, staring at Joseph's brown eyes. When Danny looks into my eyes, it's as though he is seeing deep into my soul.

Mama allowed all of my brothers to hold the baby today. Luke made me laugh by looking so nervous. He's becoming a better brother daily, just like Ben was.

Friday, October 6, 1871

Papa is preparing for the journey to sell the crops. He has to take two wagons to carry everything, so Lyle is going, too. Last year, Ben drove the other wagon. Luke and Rob will stay here to look after things. Jonah and Micah are going with Papa as well. Papa likes to go as soon as he can to get the best prices on his crops. We never know how long he will be gone, and I always miss him when he leaves. It's a part of our life, so Papa has to go.

Saturday, October 7, 1871

I awoke much earlier than usual this morning. I crept from the house to the barn, wrapped in my shawl. I sat in the hay and pondered many things. I feel much older now. Though I am fourteen, I feel that I am more mature. I also feel that I may be coming to love Rob. I think of him very often, and my heart flutters when he so much as looks at me. Perhaps one day, I will know how he feels, if he feels the same as I. I hope he does.

Sunday, October 8, 1871

We all went to church, where Reverend Wilson welcomed Joseph into the family of God. Rob sat behind me during the service. Once, he pulled my braid and I turned to look at him. He smiled, and I turned back, afraid of getting in trouble. In a few moments, my thick, curly hair suddenly unbraided. I reached my hand to feel it, and I felt Rob's hand as he handed me my ribbon. I'm not sure if it came loose on its own, or if Rob pulled it out. I tend to think it was the latter. Mama asked me, and I told her that my ribbon must have come loose. I'm sure she didn't notice Rob. As we left the church, Rob said I have pretty hair. He also asked if he could walk me home. Before I could answer, Papa called for me. I smiled at Rob and hurried to the wagon. I smiled at him as we rode away. Luke saw me, grinned, and shook his head. I believe that my secret is no longer a secret.

Monday, October 9, 1871

Papa, Lyle, Jonah, and Micah left to sell the crops today. Mama always sheds tears when she has to say good-bye to Papa. I cried a little as well, and Nora was almost distraught over having to say goodbye to Lyle. Now it's very quiet here, and lonely.

Tuesday, October 10, 1871

After I milked the cows and gathered the eggs, I went to help Luke and Rob cut the corn stalks down. It was hard work, and I was nervous around Rob. The three of us hardly spoke at all, but we did get the stalks bound into sheaves. They look very nice standing in the fields.

Wednesday, October 11, 1871

As I went to milk the cows this morning, the wind whipped around me, sending a chill down my spine. I dread the cold winter weather. Winters can be harsh on the prairie, and snow storms can last for days. I don't like to be cold; I prefer the warm summer days.

Thursday, October 12, 1871

Luke, Rob, and Danny went hunting today. This left Mama, Nora, the babies, and me alone for the day. Nora is like a sister to me. After all, she is only eighteen years old. I enjoy our time together, especially when no boys are around.

Luke killed a deer today, and it had giant antlers. It had to be cut up and stored away for winter, but I didn't have the stomach to help. I feel sick just thinking about it.

Friday, October 13, 1871

I awoke this morning to Joseph's crying. He rarely cries, but occasionally has a moment of tears. When I went into the barn, I found a handful of flowers on the milking stool. They were dry and brown, but I understand. The flowers are beginning to die. Tied with a yellow ribbon, the flowers were accompanied by a note that read, "Dear Mary, you are a lovely girl." The note rests in my diary with the others. If only the young man would sign his name to the note.

Saturday, October 14, 1871

Paul brought a letter from Ben today. I was so happy about the letter that I hardly looked at Paul. Ben wrote that all is well and happy, and he wishes he could see us all. He received our letter about Joseph's birth, and is happy to have another brother, though he hasn't even met him. I miss Ben very much.

Sunday, October 15, 1871

We went to church today. Since Papa took both of our wagons to sell the crops, we rode with the Hamiltons. After the service, Rob asked if he could walk me home. I asked Mama, who agreed with a questioning look in her eyes. Everyone else rode away in the wagon with Luke driving, leaving Rob and me alone as we began to walk. I was very shy, unsure of what to do or say. Rob seemed just as nervous, keeping silent for the first few moments. Finally, Rob broke the silence by saying that he's been thinking of me often. I blushed and told him that I've been doing the same. Rob looked at my face and laughed. We stopped walking, and he took my hands in his.

"Mary, I liked you from the very moment I first saw you standing alone on the prairie. I've never thought of anyone like I've thought of you."

My heart fluttered so, I thought I would faint. We continued walking, Rob holding my hand the entire time. When we arrived at my house, I thanked him for walking me home and for the nice things he said. I would have said something more, but the words wouldn't leave my mouth. We said goodbye, and I went into the house. My smile was enough to greet everyone. Mama smiled back and said, "Why, Mary, I had no idea you and Rob were sweet on each other!" I could think of nothing to say, and

Mama seemed to understand. I thought of Rob for the rest of the day. I feel so much older, almost like a grown woman.

Monday, October 16, 1871

We have nothing to do but prepare for winter. Luke and Danny went hunting, Rob chopped wood, and I stacked it. Papa already has our wood chopped and stacked for the winter, but the Hamiltons don't. They haven't lived on the prairie long enough to be thoroughly prepared for the winter, so we help them when we can.

Tuesday, October 17, 1871

Papa, Lyle, and the boys returned today. Everyone was very happy to see one another again. Papa was able to get very good prices for the crops, and has already settled with Lyle for his share. Papa held Joseph for the entire day, and has begun to call him Joe. I think it fits, though Mama isn't so happy. Jonah and Micah told every detail of the trip several times. I did miss them being here. I'm used to being surrounded by boys. It's lonely without them.

Wednesday, October 18, 1871

Paul and Henry Forbes rode to our farm today. They brought news that the harvest celebration will be on Friday night. Henry's family will have it at their farm since they have a large barn and plenty of room for dancing. I can't wait. I'm sure Rob will dance with me.

Thursday, October 19, 1871

This morning, I found another gift on the milking stool. This time, there were only a few flowers that looked half alive. They were tied with a violet ribbon. The note read, "I'll see you at the dance. I promise we'll dance together." Now, I have high hopes of finding out who is giving flowers to me.

Friday, October 20, 1871

It is nearly time to go to the Forbes' farm. Mama, knowing my thoughts somehow, allowed me to bathe. I am now wearing a clean dress and my hair is braided and tied with my violet ribbon. I'm holding little Joe as he sleeps, and watching as my brothers prepare under Mama's direction. I must add that Mama looks beautiful in her blue calico. It looks good with her blond hair. Papa just whispered that she is still the belle of the ball. It's nearly time to leave, so I'll write more later.

Saturday, October 21, 1871

Last night was wonderful! The Forbes' farm was lit with so many lanterns it shone like daylight. The entire community was there, from farmers to shopkeepers. The number of children is amazing. They had no interest in dancing, so they played until they fell asleep. There are only a few girls my age, but they've never paid much attention to me, so I don't know any of them very well. The rest of the young people are young men. There were couples of all ages, both married and not. Everyone had a wonderful time.

As the dancing and music began, I sat with Joe and watched as Mama and Papa danced. I couldn't help but wait to dance, hoping to discover the one who has given me flowers. Luke smiled as he sat down beside me, probably sensing what I was thinking. So when Rob asked me to dance, Luke offered to hold Joe. I shyly took Rob's hand, and we joined the dancing. I also danced with Paul, Henry Forbes, and Adam Clark. However, I danced most every dance with Rob. We reeled, jigged, and square danced. The music continued long into the night. Mama and Papa danced only with each other, as did Lyle and Nora. Lily and Joe fell asleep long before midnight, and Danny soon followed. Micah sat with the babies until he, too, was overcome by sleep. Jonah terrorized the little neighbor girls until Papa made him sit down and behave. Luke danced and seemed to enjoy himself. However, the dance was very boring for the others compared to the time I had.

I so enjoyed dancing with Rob. I admired his brown hair and green eyes. Every dance was enjoyable, and Rob was as sweet as he could be. Even when I was dancing with someone else, I would still see him watching me. After my dance with Paul, I sat down next to Papa, who was resting. He asked if I was enjoying myself, and I told him that I was. It was then that Mr. Johnson, who was playing the fiddle, announced a dance for courting couples only. Several young couples hurried to the dance floor. Rob appeared before Papa and me. "Mr. Lawson, I would like permission to court your daughter and for her to join me for a dance." Rob looked hopeful and Papa looked surprised. Papa looked at Rob, then at me, then at Rob again. He didn't seem to know how to answer. Finally, Papa answered, "You may court Mary, but I think the dance can wait." Rob looked happy, yet disappointed about the dance, which was already over by then. I smiled as he walked away, feeling very happy.

Mama returned from looking after Joe, and she and Papa returned to dancing. Nora was at my side by then, and she whispered, "Someone is outside waiting for you." She smiled mysteriously, and I curiously stepped outside the barn. I peered into the darkness. All at once, Rob took my hand and said, "We'll have our dance now if you want." Oh, I wanted to have that dance, but I couldn't make myself disobey Papa. Instead, I led Rob back to the barn where we sat together, watching the others dance. I caught Papa's eye, and he smiled and nodded. I knew he was giving his permission for Rob and me to dance. With that, Rob and I danced until dawn, when the celebration ended. I am now writing, forcing myself to stay awake and record the night's events. I've already milked the cows, so now I'm going to sleep.

Sunday, October 22, 1871

After a long rest, we awoke ready for church. When I went to milk the cows, I realized I had danced with four boys, and I still didn't know who was giving flowers to me. I thought about it all during church, hardly hearing the sermon. I wish I knew the answer to my nagging question.

Monday, October 23, 1871

I was milking the cows this morning when Luke came into the barn. He sat down near me, and I could tell he wanted to say something. I waited patiently. Finally he said, "Papa told me that you and Rob are courting." I

know I blushed, and Luke laughed. "You look very happy, and I'm happy for you." I thanked him, for I know that at times he and Rob haven't gotten along well. I hope they will in the future.

Tuesday, October 24, 1871

We received a letter from Samuel. He wrote the usual.

Papa, Rob, Lyle, and my brothers went hunting. Papa's hoping to store up a fair amount of meat for winter. He thinks it will come early this year. I wish it wouldn't.

Wednesday, October 25, 1871

Rob came to go hunting with Luke today. He and I talked until Luke was ready. I can't see what I used to dislike about Rob. However, he does still tease me a little. Any chance he gets, he pulls the ribbon from my braid. My curly hair immediately falls loose, brushing the top of my shoulders. Rob says my hair looks nice loose, but I argue that it's not practical. My hair gets in the way if I leave it loose. I think he's sweet, but I'll still braid my hair.

Thursday, October 26, 1871

Papa and Luke brought home a deer and two rabbits. I couldn't make myself help clean and preserve the meat. Mama says I'll have to learn, but I can't stand to see the inside of an animal. Most of all, I hate the emptiness of their cold, dead eyes.

Friday, October 27, 1871

Today seemed longer than usual. Rob didn't come at all.

Saturday, October 28, 1871

The entire family went into town today. We went to the general store to buy what we need for winter. In addition to flour, sugar, lantern oil, and other necessary items, we also bought cloth for new clothes. The boys don't have many choices when it comes to cloth, but Mama and I do. We never choose anything very bright. Mama chose a red calico for herself, and I chose blue gingham. We will make the dresses during the long winter days when we are trapped inside by snow. Mr. Bailey helped us find everything we needed. It may be next spring before I see town again. I enjoyed my last visit of the year. I noticed Mama glancing at some of the fine things in the store, but she never said a word. I'm sure she thought of her old home, but her look of regret and sadness is gone. Over the summer, I think Mama and I have grown closer to each other. Maybe now she doesn't resent having a daughter.

Sunday, October 29, 1871

At church today, Reverend Wilson announced that he will have services all winter, though he knows that most of the farm families will not be able to attend. The winter months are difficult when no one can leave home.

Monday, October 30, 1871

As I milked the cows, I heard the chickens cackling loudly. I thought that Calico was probably bothering them, so I waited until I was finished with the cows before I checked on the chickens. However, I was startled to find a fox clawing his way through the hens' house. I called for Papa, but the fox ran off with one of the hens before Papa arrived. He and I found only two of the hens alive, though very frightened, while the third lay dead in the straw. The poor things. Perhaps if I had checked on them sooner I could have saved the two. Papa said it wasn't my fault, but I still feel responsible.

Tuesday, October 31, 1871

Paul brought a letter from Ben. He smiled at me, though he knows Rob and I are courting. Ben wrote that he and Penny are happy and well, awaiting the arrival of their baby. I miss Ben very much, and sent a letter telling all that is happening here. He will enjoy hearing of our dull lives.

Wednesday, November 1, 1871

Mama began lessons today. She teaches us at home, as she always has. Since I have finished all of my schooling, I spend my time helping the boys with their lessons. Even though Danny can't speak, he can read and write. Mama cleverly devised a way to be sure he is learning, and he learns very quickly. Micah does well with his lessons, and, though he doesn't like them, so does Jonah. Luke is happy that he is finished with his lessons, and is set on being a farmer. He will make a good one, but one day

he'll have to have a family. He doesn't think so right now, but I'm sure the right girl will come along.

Thursday, November 2, 1871

Cold wind whipped around me as I went to the barn this morning. Papa said it could be a hard winter, as gray clouds are already gathering in the sky. Papa tied a rope from the barn to the house. He must be able to care for the animals during the snowy weather. A rope provides a means to go to the barn without becoming lost in a blizzard. Mama sent me to see if Nora needs anything for the winter. Nora needed nothing, but I stayed to visit for a while. Rob was very sweet to me, though he pulled the ribbon from my hair. For a moment, it felt as though Rob were the only other person in the room. I found myself staring at him, thinking of what things will be like in the future. I'm not sure how much time went by before Lily's cries woke me from my daydream. These thoughts followed me all day. I suddenly thought I may not see Rob for the entire winter. I hope he won't forget me. I also pray fervently that God draws us together in His care and will.

Friday, November 3, 1871

Paul brought another letter today. It was for me, from Sarah. Paul told Papa that he won't be bringing our letters during the winter, so Papa can get them when he comes to town. I hurried to the barn to be alone and tore open the letter. Sarah's words brought tears to my eyes. She wrote the usual, that she and James are well and happy. However, this time she told me where she is

because she wants me to send a letter to her. She wrote that she is lonesome, but still doesn't want her brothers to know where she is; she knew I'd keep it a secret. Now I can't tell Rob or Lyle. I wrote to Sarah, telling her how much I miss her and begging her to come home or let me tell her brothers where she is. I pray she replies soon, and in the way I want her to.

Saturday, November 4, 1871

Rob came into the barn while I was milking the cows. He sat down next to me, and I told him that Sarah had sent me a letter. I told him all that she wrote except for what she made me promise not to. However, Rob knew I was hiding something. He asked; I refused. He guessed, but incorrectly. Finally, he looked straight in my eyes and said, "Mary, you can tell me anything." That broke me, but I made him promise to keep quiet. I told him everything, and he was relieved to finally know where Sarah is. He said he would have to tell Lyle, but neither will write to her. Though I didn't keep Sarah's secret, I think I did the right thing. It also led to something wonderful. Rob and I sat in the barn and talked for hours. We talked about anything we could think of. I asked Rob if he believed in God, but his response wasn't what I expected. He said that he'd never thought about it. It made me sad, as I want to marry someone who shares my faith. I hurried to the house, grabbed my Bible from my table, and took it back to the barn. I pointed out a few specific Scriptures to Rob, and then asked him to take the Bible and read it over the winter. Perhaps he will learn a little more and give his life to God. He and I talked until nightfall, not eating one meal the entire day. We would have talked longer, but Papa came and told me it was time to come inside. I said

goodbye to Rob, and followed Papa into the house. Mama gave me a little something to eat. She said she was going to call me to lunch and supper, but didn't want to disturb us. I'm glad she didn't. I learned more about Rob, as he did about me. I don't think he will forget me through the winter. I'm sure I'll think of him often. I like him very much.

Sunday, November 5, 1871

Joseph began crying loudly during church today. Mama couldn't quiet him, so she and Papa went home early. The rest of us were to go home with the Hamiltons. After the service, my brothers climbed into Lyle's wagon. However, Rob asked to walk me home. Though it was cold outside, I agreed. As we walked, it began to snow. Soon the wind was blowing the snow hard around us. I began to fear being lost in the blizzard and freezing to death. Rob took my hand and pulled me along with him. We walked slowly, as the wind was against us. The snow stung my eyes as I tried to see the house or the barn, even though I knew we weren't even near home. It seemed to take forever to move even a few steps. As it seemed to take longer, I began to grow very worried. I grasped Rob's hand tighter as I began to stumble behind him. The wind was blowing so fiercely I could hardly stay on my feet. I fell once, but Rob pulled me up. He put his arm around me and we continued to walk. He yelled above the wind, "We should learn not to get caught in storms like this!" I laughed, and I knew we would be safe. I took Rob's hand, and asked him to pray with me. He agreed, and I said a simple prayer for God to protect us and guide us home. The wind blew colder and the snow fell harder. I was beginning to lose hope when Rob pointed out a light in the distance. I knew that Papa had hung a lantern outside to guide us. I thanked God with all my heart. Rob held me closer and said, "I'm glad your faith is strong." I eagerly pulled Rob along as we hurried toward the light. We pushed open the door, a swirl of snow following us into the house. The cries of joy from my family overwhelmed us. Mama wrapped her arms around me and hurried me to the fireplace. Rob was going to go home, but Papa said, "You'll never make it in this storm. Stay here for the night, son." I was surprised to hear Papa call Rob "son." As Mama helped me into dry clothes in my room, she said that she and Papa approve of Rob. I was so cold I couldn't respond. Mama wrapped me in a blanket and led me to sit by the fire. Rob was there in dry clothes, and my brothers crowded around to hear what happened. I realized that it had taken Rob and me nearly five hours to walk three miles. I think we walked in circles instead of in a straight line to get home. Mama gave us some warm soup while we told what had happened. I'm worn out from the adventure, but I can't sleep because of the excitement I feel. I was nearly lost in a blizzard, but God gave me the strength to be brave, and I am fine. Rob is sleeping upstairs; I'm sure Lyle and Nora are worried about him. Together, Rob and I have survived a tornado and a blizzard. I'm sure we could make it through anything together.

Monday, November 6, 1871

It took a very long time for me to get warm last night. This morning, I dressed quickly against the cold. The warm stove drew me in that direction. I pulled on my coat and scarf, but Papa snatched my hat from my hand.

"I'll milk the cows this morning. You stay warm,"

he told me. Papa headed out into the snow, and Mama served breakfast. Rob prepared to go home, and Luke went with him. The snow had stopped falling, though nearly two feet of it covered the ground. Luke reported that Lyle and Nora had been worried sick, and were very happy to have Rob home safe and to know that I was safe as well. I'm happy, too.

Tuesday, November 7, 1871

It seems that winter has come early this year. It snowed all day long. Papa thinks it will be a long storm.

Wednesday, November 8, 1871

Another day of snow and being trapped in the house. Papa won't let me go milk the cows yet. Though I've never felt this way before, I'm very restless. I believe that the events of this summer have changed me. I don't feel as timid as I used to. I'm still shy, but I've gained the ability to speak up and be braver than usual. The winter will prove if it is a phase, or a true change.

Thursday, November 9, 1871

This was another day of snow. Midway through the afternoon, things became difficult. Jonah was tired of doing lessons, Micah was tired, and Joe was crying. Mama was at her wit's end, but Papa came to the rescue. He was standing by the window, his arms folded, when he began speaking in his deep, soft voice.

"It was a snowy day like this," he began. "We had been fighting for days, but the cold wind drove us to seek shelter. Me and another boy, we were scouts. We went out and couldn't seem to find our unit. Me and Sam, my partner, we found this little clearing in the woods. Thinking it better to stay warm than become two frozen scouts, we built a fire and settled down for the night. We were nearly asleep when we heard someone crashing through the woods. Sam and I grabbed our rifles and prepared to go down fighting." Papa paused here, turning to look at his captivated audience. The room was silent except for the crackling fire. Even Mama listened with interest and Joe was silent as well. Papa sat down at the table and continued.

"Sam and I waited for an entire army to walk through the brush. Our rifles were leveled, ready to fire. Finally, two Yankee soldiers, scouts like us, stepped through the brush. They leveled their guns, and we stared at each other a long time."

"Did you shoot them?" Jonah asked eagerly.

"We all stared at one another," Papa said, ignoring Jonah's question. "One of the Yankees finally said, 'We saw your fire and thought maybe we could find a little shelter.' I looked at Sam, and he at me, and we lowered our rifles. The Yankees lowered theirs, and we gathered around the fire. Soon, we were telling stories about our families and homes. I remember that Danny had just been born, and I was the man with the most children. We slept well, not at all wary of our enemy company. At times like that, no one cared what side you were on. We shook hands the next morning and parted company. I don't think I ever saw those two men again."

Papa had a faraway look in his eyes. He told many stories today. I've never heard Papa talk about the war. It was a special day. When Micah asked him what the worst part of the war was, I could tell that Papa had thought about that question many times. "Most men would say the noise was the worst, the noise of the battle, the sounds of war. But they're wrong. The worst part was the silence. After a battle, a hush would fall over the field, broken only by the stench of death. It was during the silent times that a man's mind would wander home, to the people he loves. Silence was the hardest battle to fight. I would rather face a whole army alone than face a dead silence that engulfed me without relief."

Papa's eyes revealed the depth of his soul. I saw his heart today, though he never keeps it hidden from us. It was a day that would never be repeated.

Friday, November 10, 1871

It finally stopped snowing today. Papa let me go with him to the barn. We waded through the snow, holding the rope to steady ourselves. The snow soaked through my skirt easily, and I was chilled to the bone by the time we reached the barn. Bess and Ann greeted me warmly, and I rubbed their backs, telling them that I had missed them. Luke laughed at me as he came to help Papa. They cared for the horses as I milked the cows. The cows' warm bodies penetrated the cold, and I tried to warm my hands before I milked them. The milk caused steam to rise from the frozen buckets. Calico sat at my feet as I worked. She looked at me with pitiful eyes, and I felt very sorry for her. Papa took care of the milk, and I looked in on the horses, especially my favorite mare, the one who lost the foal. With Papa's permission, I took Calico into the house, wrapped warmly in my coat as I carried her close to me. Danny was delighted to see her as he loves her very much.

Mama didn't quite approve, but tolerated the cat with a small bowl of cream. I think she likes Calico more than she would ever admit. It was a fairly quiet day, with no visit from Rob.

Saturday, November 11, 1871

I only have a few pages left in my diary. I asked Papa if he could perhaps get some paper from town for me. He responded, "Mary, I would be happy to get it, since you never ask me for anything, but I'm not sure if we can afford it." Papa wants to be sure that our money will last through the winter. He wants to be sure that we have enough supplies, and I agree. My paper can wait.

Sunday, November 12, 1871

We didn't go to church today. The snow is too deep to drive the wagon through. Since our adventure last Sunday, Rob didn't come to visit. I still miss him, though. This will be a long winter.

Monday, November 13, 1871

I have only three pages to record a great event on. Mid-morning, we heard a ringing of sleigh bells. Papa opened the door, and then beckoned me to come. I looked out and saw Rob in a sleigh. He asked Papa if I could go riding with him. I waited breathlessly, and Papa agreed. I quickly pulled on my coat, hat, gloves, and scarf, and hurried out to the sleigh. I waved to my brothers, who were watching from the door as Rob gave me his hand. I climbed into the sleigh and we set off. Rob explained that

he borrowed the sleigh from the Forbes family just so we could go riding. We had a wonderful time, even though the cold air burned my cheeks. When Rob drove across the bridge, he said that he had to collect a toll. A toll is a kiss. When I learned this, I stoutly refused. I told him I would kiss no one until the day I married him. Rob thought it was a good idea, and didn't cross the bridge again until he took me home. It felt wonderful to be outside, to breathe the fresh air. Rob was sweet as always, and took me home a little after noon. He said he would see me again soon, but I'm not sure if the weather will allow it. However, the more time I spend with Rob, the more

Monday, February 5, 1872

It has been months since my last entry, but something terrible happened that prevented me from writing. It all happened very quickly, but I remember every detail. I was writing at the table by the fire. Papa came inside after closing up the barn for the night. As he hung up his coat, he stepped on Calico's tail. Calico yowled and ran across the room. She ran right under Mama's feet, causing her to drop the pot she was drying. The crash startled Micah, who was very interested in a book just then. Micah jumped, throwing the book, which hit my hand, sending my pencil flying into the fire. We didn't have another pencil or pen in the house. Therefore, I haven't been able to write until now. The winter has passed slowly, with no unusual activity. I've only seen Rob twice. I miss him. We went to town today, as the weather allowed it. Papa made sure I had paper and pencils, which was very nice of him. We are now a little low on money, and I feel guilty that I have something as unimportant as paper and pencils. However, now I am able to finish the last line of my last entry: *I like him.*

Tuesday, February 6, 1872

Though it's still cold, it didn't snow today. I can't wait for spring to arrive.

Wednesday, February 7, 1872

Mama and I spent the day sewing, as we have many days this winter. My quilt is growing larger, and looks good. Mama finished her dress today. I told her it was very nice, and she said it would be better with lace. We have none, and I know Mama won't ask for any. I'm going to try to get some for her. I can't make any myself, or I would. Perhaps I'll think of something before we go to town again.

Thursday, February 8, 1872

Papa sent Luke into town to mail letters, and I went with him. No one knows it, but I had my copy of *Little Women* tucked inside my coat. While Luke mailed the letters, I took my book to the general store. I quickly picked some lace, and asked Mr. Bailey if I could trade the book for it. He looked at me questioningly, but agreed to the trade. I asked him to keep it a secret, tucking the lace into my pocket. Luke came to get me then, and we went home. When I had a chance, I slipped the lace into Mama's sewing basket. I hope she finds it soon.

Friday, February 9, 1872

Mama didn't sew today, so she didn't find the lace. I'm growing impatient and eager. Lace is one of Mama's favorite things. She told me once that she had a dress that was covered from top to bottom in beautiful, expensive white lace. It was her favorite dress, and she left it behind when she left home. She hasn't had a dress with lace since then. Now she will have one.

Saturday, February 10, 1872

I found a lonesome note on the milking stool today, the first since Rob and I began courting. The note read, "Sweet Mary, I love you more daily." I hurried outside, looking for tracks in the snow. I found a set of horse tracks, heading toward the prairie, away from anyone I know. Who on earth could be responsible for these gifts?

Sunday, February 11, 1872

Mama, Joe, and Danny stayed home from church while the rest of us made the journey. It was a dull service, but I still listened. Afterward, Rob asked to walk me home. Papa took a good look at the sky, then smiled and agreed. As Rob and I walked, he handed me my Bible from his coat pocket.

"I read a lot over the winter," he said. "I learned a lot, and decided that I wanted the kind of faith you have."

I was so happy I threw my arms around his neck. Since Rob is taller than I am, I had to reach up to hug him. He seemed very happy as well, and I thanked God through my tears of joy. Rob does seem different. He seems changed. I enjoyed our walk, the longest amount of time we've spent together all winter. I look forward to more walks as spring will soon be approaching.

Monday, February 12, 1872
My visions of spring have faded; snow once again covered the ground this morning. Mama still hasn't found her lace.

Tuesday, February 13, 1872
I sat down and began sewing today, hoping Mama would do the same. She did, and pulled her newly finished dress from her basket. The roll of lace fell to the floor. Mama bent to pick it up, her eyes shining in amazement. She struggled to say something, but succeeded only in beginning to cry. I fought to keep my eyes from betraying my secret. Mama turned to Papa, thinking that he had bought the lace. He looked surprised, too, but I think Mama still thinks he bought it. Mama wiped her eyes, and said, "Thank you!" My heart swelled until I thought it would burst! I couldn't help but smile for the rest of the day.

Wednesday, February 14, 1872
I went to milk the cows early this morning. I was soon joined by Rob, to my surprise. His eyes shone with a secret, and he sat next to me as I milked the cows. I asked him what he was smiling about, and he said he had something for me. He didn't wait for my response, but eagerly pulled a brown package from his coat. I opened it carefully, and found my copy of *Little Women*. I was speechless, but able to ask how he knew. "I saw you the day you got the lace for your mother. I knew you were giving up something that was special to you, and I wanted you to have it back." I nearly cried; it was so special and

thoughtful. I went back to milking to hold in my tears. It was then that I focused on the brown paper. Written in a familiar hand were the words, "For Mary, With Love." I realized at that moment it had been Rob all along who gave me flowers all summer. I caught my breath, and asked Rob if it had been him, just to be sure. He confessed that it had been, and he had no other words to say how he felt. I felt my heart flutter uncontrollably, and Rob and I stared into each other's eyes. I believe we both felt that we will love each other forever. Rob squeezed my hand as he left. I turned back to milking and sighed. My love-struck moment was cut short as Rob pulled the ribbon from my braid. He laughed and tossed my ribbon to me. I shook my head as he disappeared, but I love him still the same.

For today, I let my hair hang loose.

TATE PUBLISHING & *Enterprises*

Tate Publishing is commited to excellence in the publishing industry. Our staff of highly trained professionals, including editors, graphic designers, and marketing personnel, work together to produce the very finest books available. The company reflects the philosophy established by the founders, based on Psalms 68:11,

"THE LORD GAVE THE WORD AND GREAT WAS THE COMPANY OF THOSE WHO PUBLISHED IT."

If you would like further information, please call
1.888.361.9473
or visit our website
www.tatepublishing.com

TATE PUBLISHING & *Enterprises*, LLC
127 E. Trade Center Terrace
Mustang, Oklahoma 73064 USA